Aeverless 3.2

Jones Harwell

Aeverless 3.2

Illustrations by Rhayven Jones

Published by Redbaby Publishing, Inc., Clinton, MD, 20735.

ISBN 978-1-952163-04-3 eBook

ISBN 978-1-952163-05-0 Paperback

Dedication

Thank you, my heavenly Father, for continuing to give me stories to tell. Avery, my heart and partner in life, thank you for walking in this journey with me and continuing to push me to pursue my dreams. To my kids, Aleah and JeLan, and my grandkids, thanks for the giggles, the life lessons and the privilege of being your momma. To my parents, siblings, aunts, uncles and cousins, you are the foundation which Avery and I lean on. Thank you for your undying love and support.

My sisters (Karla, Donna, DaRell, Kisha, Iris and LaTicia) you keep me grounded, laughing and as real as I can be. I could not have asked for a better group of sister friends in this lifetime.

To you the reader, inside these pages I share with you my imagination. What starts as a blank page quickly becomes a canvas and I hope the words and scenery challenge you to think beyond this reality and see the world, Aeverless 3.2.

"Every war, when it comes, or before it comes, is represented not as a war but as an act of self-defense against a homicidal maniac."

George Orwell

Current Day

"Record. Journal entry May 19, 2278. Half of the day is already behind me and I have two to three more hours to find shelter before dusk. It is not safe out here, in the middle of nowhere, with nothing but highway and desert for as long as I can see. My last place of shelter lasted for four days, and that was pushing it. Survival requires constant busy. I do not stay in one place for over three days. Between the wild and the zombies, you are better off in motion. The wild comes out during the day with temperatures sometimes peaking between 115-125 degrees. Between the zombies and frigid weather, nighttime becomes your best friend." I place the recorder back in my pocket. I curse myself for miscalculating the heat. My car has been sucking coolant for the past hour and has now shut down. After spending the last few minutes camouflaging my ride, I venture southwest from its location in search of water and or shelter. I take all my belongings with me, for I have no choice. I do not want to run into anything living that is looking for me to be their next meal. Water. Shelter. Survival. My map does not show this area at all. If I had to venture a guess, I think I reached the tip of what used to be Oklahoma, which borders Colorado and Texas.

I am still a long way from the territory of ancient ancestors called Guatemala. The last strong transmission from six months ago stated there is a secure post and ships at sea harboring safety from the elements. This terrain is not like any I have seen since I started my journey. I tread lightly as the ground cover is as thick as the trees, an eerie shade of deep green with black moss. There is a smell of decay and death about. This is not a good sign. I continue my trek, eyes darting front, side to side, looking for any motion. Snap! I scream out in pain. Wrong move, man. If anything is out here, they know you are here now. Failing to look down, I stepped right into a steel trap. Effective measure as I look back up into the bunt of a weapon that knocks me out cold.

Quickly, the young woman throws a blanket of deep green and black moss over the man she just rendered immobile. Senses heighten, she works swiftly. After many months alone, the alarm sounded out of the blue. She had started not to respond at all, figuring it was a rabid animal caught in a trap, however the sensor determined the culprit was human. She has not been this far from the complex in quite some time. Spotting his vehicle, she frisks it, retrieving some items before covering it with a more effective camouflage that would render any followers immobile temporarily. Making her way back to the man, removes his ankle from the trap and wraps it with a bandage. With great strength she loads him onto her sleigh-like vehicle, and with the speed of a jaguar they move through the vegetation without making a sound. Within several minutes, she reaches her destination at the garage. Entering from the east, she opens the first steel grid. Easing the sleigh into the sewage pipe, she turns and secures the grid, and then pulls another steel grid down from the top of the pipe, repeating the process. This is the first line of defense. Moving again with great speed, she has only another thirty minutes to get to her destination. After maneuvering several turns through the pipes, she comes to a dead end. Removing the debris, she uncovers a steel door with a decipher lock. Entering a code, she places her left hand to the right of the door. It opens. Remounting the sleigh, she enters debunks and pulls the door closed behind her. She checks her stopwatch, 00:15:00. Fifteen minutes to spare before dust makes its descent on the world outside. Adjusting her mask, she places a spare mask on the man and covers the sleigh with a protective cover. She waits as a fine mist falls from the atmosphere. Once it clears, she drives ahead another fifty feet with its unconscious cargo to the waiting elevator. "Argo, open please."

"Welcome back, Brooks. What floor please?"

"Six,"

"I detect you are not alone."

"No, I found a stray in the woods. Once I get him to the lab, let us keep him out for a little longer while we find out more about him."

A few seconds later, the elevator opens to the sixth floor. Its appearance is in huge contrast to the floor leading out to the sewage pipes. The sewage entrance is rusty, designed to detour anything walking or crawling inhibiting its space. They design the mist to kill anything living object on site, requiring the use of the mask. The sixth floor is quite open and divided by glass like walls into three sections. To the far left appears to be a clinic area, with the center being sterile and the right filled with ten rows of electronics from servers to security cameras and more. Pulling the sleigh into the center room, a door closes behind them. Shower heads emerge from the walls on both sides of her. She undresses the man and herself, placing the clothing in a container resembling a trash chute that has appeared at the back of the room. Pressing the wall above it, it retreats into the wall. The clothes burn. She moves the man to the right of the room, careful not to touch the walls. She collects the remaining of his belongings and places on the wall opposite of the trash chute onto a conveyor belt, which disappears once she walks away. On the left, she taps the wall above the far-left showerhead and showers. Tapping again, the showerhead retreats and opens a panel in the center. She dresses and exits the room, making her way to the room of cameras and devices.

Sitting at a display of monitors labeled for each floor, she reviews the footage before. Satisfied that they are safe for the moment, she redirects her attention to the man on the floor. He resembles the man from her dreams. For months, recurring dreams plagued her. Faces and places unfamiliar. This was the only home she knew. After months, years of silence, she hoped that there were others, like her in the world. She thought she was alone until now. She had people in her dreams, her imagination to keep her company. Until today, when he appeared out of nowhere. Her dad had warned her. Told her that there would come a time when she would need to make split second judgements. Now the time is upon her. Trust or not. Leaving him in the woods would present a new set of problems. Bringing him here presents problems. Her visions alluded to him traveling with her to places far beyond this facility. Trusting her father's words, she turned off the security, went through the maze and brought him here.

Argo had already inspected his belongings and had the items laid on the table before her. Her visitor traveled light. A stopwatch, a couple of metal objects that resemble keys, a journal, a tape recorder, some writing materials, some tools, a couple of knives and a gun with ammo. Thumbing through the journal, it looks he kept a daily account of the terrain he traveled across and pictured in the front was a rough map of what they once called The Americas. Circled was the country known as Guatemala. Nothing showed his name or how old he was. She suspected they were close in age, maybe one of them older than the other by only a few years. Inspecting the man again, she notes Argo has also finished a preliminary physical. Charcoal, his height was just shy of six foot four. Great muscle tone, which meant he takes great care of his body. Lean, which meant he might have some speed to him. No missing teeth, no signs of contaminated blood, no other physical scars or marks other than the teeth of the steel trap which will disappear in a few more days. "I've already given him the disinfectants. Shall I wake him?"

"Yes, Argo, turn on the water so our guest can bathe, please. When he's finished, lead him to the third floor."

~

"What the hell," as he jumps up from the white floor to warm water streaming out of the walls. Shaking away the cobwebs, he turns about to get his bearings. The room was devoid of furniture, just the water streaming from what seem to be faucets on the wall. Standing for several moments, he wonders if he is dreaming. It had been a while since he had use of a shower. After a few minutes, he assumes that the water is clean of germs. On a ledge is a bar of soap and a small plastic dish with a white powder labeled baking soda. He cleans his body and uses the baking soda to clean his mouth. Stepping away from the faucets, they shut off and disappear into the wall. That is interesting, he surmises. A panel opens with what appears to be clean clothing. He dresses, noting an absence of shoes and a belt. The clothing fit him, as if his donor knew his exact size. Nothing fit snug or too loose. The room, well lit, is void of furniture and accessories. He suspected that some type of technology was in use but noticed no visible signs of cameras. His instincts though were telling him he was being watched. The door to the space opens, and he exits the room. Judging by the size of the hall, he found out that the space was quite large, however, I only gave him sight to the space before him. He concluded that whoever was his benefactor was not quite ready to share information on where they were located or in what. His belongings were not in the room he exited, also giving him no idea or clue to the time and how long he had been unconscious. One curious note was how his ankle healed from the trap that snared him.

Following the light, it enlightens him as a voice speaks from speakers he cannot locate. His path takes him to an open elevator. He steps in. Glancing at the panel, he notices no numbers to select from, just a space for some type of keycard entry, perhaps. The door closes, and he continued to listen to the female voice. The motion of the doors closes smoothly. He listens for the gears to give him a sign to whether it is moving up or down.

"Welcome to the town of Aeverless. Nestled in these mountains is a throwback to small towns of old. If you blink too hard, you will miss it. For there are only four principal streets, Northside, Westside, Southside and you guessed it Eastside. Northside is what we call our main business district. The bank, cleaners and two general stores occupy the mile-long road. On Eastside, Ms. Joy's Diner and Callie's Bed and Breakfast are the only tenants. Southside is the busiest with the gas station and garage owned by the Mootles family. They also own the movie theater and pool hall. That leaves

Westside, home to our local post office, court, police and law office. The courthouse has a small local office that manages the utilities."

The female pauses for a second before continuing, "If one were to look for this town on any map, they would not find it. It is just that small. Most folks only learn about it because they missed a turn on the major highway, looking for gas or a quick bite. That is the way the town folks liked it. The day of the bombings came as no shock, but we were not ready. When the sirens stopped, the infrastructure was so frayed, it prepared no one for the massive storm that followed. My family fled New York with a few neighbors and we just kept heading west. The year was 2262, and I was four years old. The devastation we saw along the way was horrific. What started as everyone pulling together to help their neighbor turned sideways. Power hungry folks who had wielded that power became elite again, resuming a class structure of the have and have nots. My family kept its head down and kept moving west. Our goal was to reach the west coast, maybe San Diego or some coastal area of Southern California. We made it as far as New Mexico. I did not think New Mexico had mountains, but there are mountains. Our transportation broke down, leaving us to walk. Hence our finding the town. My family, thinking we would stay only a day or two, found between the storm and the war life as we knew it was about to get unstable. It was not safe to travel at night and during the day, well I did not know which fear was worst. Thinking we would be okay, we stayed. However, this town was not as it appeared to be."

The doors to the elevator open and he stares down the barrel of a twelve-gauge shotgun with the most incredible brown eyes and full head of onyx curls he has ever seen staring dead back at him.

"I'm sorry I'm getting ahead of myself. My name is Brooks Coveia and I am the last living survivor in Aeverless." "What's your name?"

He cannot help himself. Was it a fact that he had not seen another human, much less a woman in more than a year? He stood there taking in the view. She must be somewhere in between 5'5 to 5'8, thin but curvy in all the right places, with the skin tone resembling a juicy piece of dark caramel. When she opened her mouth, her teeth were pure white. Amazing. He felt a stir in his loins, but closed his mind and body to those thoughts. His priority was to find out where he was and who or what she was.

"Are you finished gawking? Name?" she commands again. This time the brown of her eyes glared and darkened, like an oncoming tsunami.

"No, I'm not. I am enjoying the view. It's been a while since I have seen a woman. Even angry you're quite pretty."

"Even angry, I'm deadly. Name." Relaxing his stance, he laughs. She, however, does not budge. Her voice does a number to his pulse. It stirs at his heart and loins. A longing he has never known overcomes him. Damn, this is not the time to show any emotions, he cautions himself. "I'm sorry, even angry your voice," he starts, "is music to my ears. I am Alexander Whitehouse. Nice to meet you, Brooks Coveia." Eyes still darkened; she lowers the gun.

"We don't get many visitors,"

"We? You mentioned you were the last survivor here, or was that a lie?"

From the shadows, three bodies appear. At first glance they looked to be human, but the tell-tell sign was there, a stiffness in their gait and the pastiness in their skin tone. AI's, artificial intelligence robots, two men and a woman. The tallest stepped forward. "I'm Argo, Brooks protector." The other two remain silent.

"From your description of Aeverless, am I to assume we are in a space that Aeverless did not advertise or did this come after the war?"

"A bit of both," Brooks explained. "A lesser-known fact about Aeverless is that it was a deep cover for some military operations. The top of this building is over 20 feet below ground and encompasses the size of a professional football stadium, including seats and pavilion."

"Seeing that you are comfortable sharing some information with me, what makes you so sure I'm alone or not contaminated," he continues.

"I checked your blood and there are security measures in place. However, with your appearance here, we will need to continue to check your transportation or attempt to get rid of it. The last thing we need is unwanted guests of any kind."

"Agreed. How long have I been here?" he inquired.

"About four hours. In the morning we will go back to your vehicle and salvage what we can. There is no way to move it without leaving a trail back here, which is not advisable. If you are hungry, let us eat. I'll show you the facility. We can plan how to proceed from here." Alexander follows Brooks as she gives him the layout of what he learns to be floors three through six. He suspects there are more, but for the time acknowledges what she has shared. Starting with the sixth floor, he learns there is a fully equipped medical lab, quarantine area, and security. He found it interesting that each floor had a security section, but the section on the sixth floor seems to be the major hub. We divided floor five into two sections, a library or maybe a teaching facility, and another security hub. The fourth floor also had a security hub, along with a spacious living quarter, complete with a full gym, pool, and sauna and theater room. The lightening and décor made the residents feel both an indoor and outdoor ambience. It was quite impressive and from all indications took more elbow grease and hard work. Outside of Argo and the other two AIs he met, he wondered if there were more AI's on the premise. Before heading to the next floor, he asks a question.

"You mentioned you are the last living survivor of Aeverless. Did everyone live on the same floor?"

"No, they redesigned this section out of necessity. Prior to moving to this facility, we lived in the houses in town. This facility housed two hundred people at its peak, comfortably. So, in answering your question yes, this building is larger than what you are getting the initial tour of. You understand why, don't you?"

He had to give it to her. Brooks is extremely intuitive and very guarded. He would have taken the same approach, maybe after observing her for a week. He prodded further. "Why didn't you observe me longer to see if I am a threat potential?"

She stops and turns towards him, giving him her full attention. "It would have been a waste of time. Observation from a far is not the same as in proximity. Up close, I get to see the real you. Body, quirks, facial expressions and all. To answer your second question, are there other AIs on the facility, I'll leave that to your imagination for now."

How the hell? What the hell? Unless she is an AI herself. He stops as he sees Brooks studying him intently. It was as if her eyes bore straight to his soul. Finally breaking her gaze, she smiles. "No, I'm not an AI. I am one hundred percent human. There are training programs at the library that keep me ready for as many real-life possibilities. When I think you are ready, you can train as there as well. I suspect there is more to you that meets the eye. I believe you can quite react and do anything necessary to stay alive. Playing possum while I carried you through the tunnel was quite ingenious."

He nods, confirming her last comment. "What gave me away and how were you able to render me unconscious again?"

"Your heartbeat sped up. If you were truly immobile, it would have remained the same. I apologize for the gas as the second punch. You must be able to react fast. As you already know, our life depends on it."

"I'll take that explanation for now as I see I will have to gain your confidence."

Reaching the kitchen, she taps the oven and types. Explaining that it should take about 30 minutes before the meal would be complete, she asks Alexander to tell her more about himself. They talk some more during dinner, and then she gives him a tour of the third floor. The entire floor was an outdoor paradise, complete with gardens, several greenhouses, and an outdoor park complete with riding trails, ponds and a beach area.

"Wow. The technology to build all of this. Impressive. Was most of this completed prior to moving in, or did more structural work need completing?"

"They finished the majority before we arrived. The town wanted to be ready if and once the time came to retreat. From what you have told me of your travels, it does not sound like other towns or cities did not think along those lines either. It's like the world lived in denial that we could function above ground following a mass destructive act."

Taking it all in, he realized that on this floor, if there was a security hub, it was not readily identifiable. They make their way make to the elevator in silence and proceed back to the living quarters. Escorting him to his private quarters, she explains he has access only to the floors they toured, and he could further examine them at his leisure. Before retreating she points out that in the living quarters, the rooms do not have security on them, but each has an intercom system. In case of emergencies, she explains the need to have immediate access to each other.

"When do we get to talk about Argo, the AI's and security," he interrupts. "That," Brooks smiles sweetly, "depends on how quick I can trust you. Good night Alexander." From his doorway, he watches her walk down the hall about hundred feet before she places her hand on the wall and disappears. Turning, he scans his quarters. Amazingly, the space resembles a nice size condo. There is a living space complete with a kitchen and lounging area, before walking into another room designated for sleeping and bathing. Checking the drawers and closets, he sees that clothing and shoes, about four days' worth, are available. Each piece completely suitable for any terrain and weather. He lays across the bed with a mind full of questions. He rewound the events from the past few days in his mind. Something had clearly spooked him on the road. That was his reason for travelling at the speed of sound. That caused him to make a critical error and losing his vehicle. How he wished he had more time. Time would allow him the opportunity to slowing get to know Brooks and determine if she is completely trustworthy. However, time was not a commodity today or any day. Between the animals, the undead, and the drastic weather mood swings, shelter is hard to find and sane humans even harder. Staring at the ceiling, he calmly rests his mind and then closes his eyes. He had to determine quickly if she was worthy of his trust, for she already saved his life once. Tomorrow is a new day, and he had still to learn and life-changing decisions to make.

From her room, Brooks watches the monitor as Alexander finally drifts into sleep. A few things puzzled her from his encounter. His car had drifted onto radar ten miles from the first security marker. Tomorrow she must find time to ensure that it is still fully functional. One element she had learned from her parents and the town council was the first line of defense was outer defense. Knowing when something or someone is close to it. Once broken, it decreases the time you have for escape if the threat potential is too great. She will keep him occupied for a few days while she checks this out. If he came with others, they could not last for over three days in the wilderness. God forbid if they are lucky enough to make it to town. Then she estimated she had another three to four days before they breach the next security perimeter. If there are no threats after ten days, she would reveal a little more. While she wished she had time, she knew at any moment it would elude her, leaving her with hard decisions to make. They designed the sensor marking his arrival not to detect mistakes; instead, it was too ready her for action, for battle.

Having no encounters with another human in over two years, she quickly shrugged off the stirring in her belly. Every instinct was telling her she could trust him, but staying alive relied on more than instincts. Common sense and strategic planning also play crucial roles. From their conversation, she learned Alexander was only months older than her. He was from Chicagoland, where he was the oldest of five children. After the war, for a while his family could stay put, but eventually with the plague and undead, they make their migration west heading for Oregon. The undead attacked the caravan, leaving Alexander as the sole survivor of his family. Another family took him in, and they made their way to Montana. He joined with a group of individuals that had firm knowledge that off the shores of Guatemala, a colony had set up camp on ships that were quite stable. He volunteered along with two others to seek it out. Each set out in a different direction. If they made it and had access to technology, they could relay a signal back and set up communication. She would have to consider that more humans might head her way. How would she handle it? The nightly dreams were warning her of things to come. She knew her time here was growing short.

"Brooks?"

"Yes, Argo,"

"We can extend the observation past ten days if needed."

"I realize that, but my dreams are coming more frequently, and I feel we may run out of time. Tomorrow insert the chips in both of us and set your safety protocol. If nothing comes our way during the next ten days, I will reveal as much as I can accept the knowledge of the chip and the other facilities like this one. We have had no contact from Abilene or Baylift City in over two months. We have calculated for every scenario, every risk. With him here, I will not risk staying past four months more. Whatever breached the security at those two locations is on its way here. Ten days will tell me if he is the mole, or it is still unknown. If the chip proves he is a walking time bomb, then neither of us will leave here or remain alive. I am going to get some rest now. Wake me at four to run security sweeps with you."

~

Morning came earlier as Brooks made her way back to the security perimeter and the location of Alexander's vehicle. Confirming that the cameras were still secure, her joy was short-lived upon inspecting the vehicle. There was a puncture in the undercarriage causing the fluid leaks. She stripped as many spare parts as she could and then created serious damage to the bones of the utility vehicle, leaving nothing for scavengers to use; giving them no reason to scout the area any further. At the last minute, she changed her route back to the facility. Call it sixth sense, but during the last twenty minutes all her senses went on high alert. What should have taken twenty-five minutes before she spent an extra fifty returning, each few kilometers laying mist to cover her trail? As an additional measure, she entered the tunnel from the town's bank. She went through the same ritual as the previous day, allowing the mist to kill off the scent and any other contaminants she made have picked up along the way. Stopping on the eighth floor, she left the parts for the Ais to dispose or strengthen for future use. Here were a couple of all-terrain vehicles and her baby. History books had referred to the vehicle as a large model sport utility vehicle. She and Argo had lovingly reinforced the vehicle from the undercarriage to the roof, leaving nothing to chance. Adding another four feet to the back allowed for extra fuel, night vision and camouflage. If she ever had to leave in a hurry, she could go twelve hundred miles in any direction and hide in plain sight if needed. Hopefully, she could get to another underground facility for shelter before that so she could produce more fuel and make any repairs if needed. With sunset falling after securing the parts, she stopped at the main security hub to review the latest footage. "Damn, who the fuck are they," she murmurs as three shadows appeared on screen. One was inspecting the vehicle and the other two were scouring the forest, stopping short of the first line of external detection. They retreat and return to the vehicle. Brooks exhales a deep sigh of relief. This time they failed. But now she has a problem. The time she thought she had had vanished, and decisions about what to do with her guest could no longer wait. "Argo, we have a problem."

~

With the setting of the sun in the forest, the shadows regrouped at the sight of the vehicle to review their notes. Spreading throughout the area, they search quickly. There was another human here besides the one they were tracking. Whoever it was, they surmised, is extremely tactical. Despite their best efforts to finding the human's sanctuary, they were unsuccessful. If they had spooked the human, they were good at showing no fear or simply had ingrained themselves to always take extra precautions. It was as if they had simply vanished. No above ground camp meant somewhere there were tunnels and a possible underground hideaway. Two scouts set off back on the main road to get reinforcements as one makes camp in the trees.

Brooks returns to the eighth floor and re-examines the salvage she brought back with her. Although valuable, it was now useless. She takes it all to the incinerator and watches every piece disintegrate. As another precaution, she puts on her mask, closes the vents and sterilizes the room. They had planned if something went wrong, she would destroy the materials before any more damage occurred. While she is accomplishing this, Argo set off the same sterilization procedure in the tunnels leading to the garage and the bank. During the rainstorm slated to start within the next two hours, he would release more mist in the forest behind the security perimeters as an extra precaution. Brooks, completely her task, rejoins Argo at the security hub. Argo reviews the new footage, while Brooks reviews yesterday footage again. After dark, the shadows had appeared in the woods, meaning they had been tracking Alexander. She replays each conversation. Finding no chips implanted somewhere in his travels, he stumbled upon these shadows. Whatever they are, they are dangerous and the more they discover about them, the better chances they have of staying alive.

"What's your next move Brooks," Argo inquires. She asks him to retrieve the footage of their guest today from the time he went to sleep last night until now. They watch in silence as he retraced every step of yesterday's tour. He must have a photogenic memory to know the complete layout for over twenty thousand feet of square footage. She chuckles as she watched him examine the walls, counter space and elevators, trying to determine or discover where the hidden cameras and speaker equipment is located.

"We may or may not have that window, as I thought. It is best I decide has to trust him for now and plan for evacuation if it comes to that. Put the protocol program in place. I will go check in our guest. Did you implant the chip?"

"Yes, I did. And before you go," Argo pauses and waits for Brooks to remove her foot covering. She does so quickly and leans forward, allowing Argo to implant the chip in between the third and fourth toe. She then heads out towards the library to meet up with Alexander.

Trusting that he did not have to sleep with one eye open, Alexander took full advantage of getting a good night's sleep. He did not know when the opportunity would come again. Lying in bed, he looked around his surroundings again. A great deal of care went into making the space feel warm and inviting, with sprinkles of nostalgia and the present era. He rises, rinses his face and mouth, and changes to an outfit left in the closet for him. Deciding not to have a bite to eat in the general area, he grabs a couple of pieces of fruit from the refrigerator in his room. He exits and makes mental notes of his current location with where the security hubs were on the floors he had access to. None were quite on top of the other, meaning there was some extensive infrastructure in this place. A lot of planning and detail went into not giving any advantages to someone thinking to breach the place. He made his way to the elevator bank. When asked where he wanted to go, he mentions the library. Less than a minute the doors open, and he made his way through the small atrium to the major bank of monitors and seating. A minor fact he did not mention to Brooks was that he was born with the ability to memorize any location, fact, or detail within seconds.

The monitor screen illuminates. A keyboard and mic sit on the left of the monitor, ready for his command. Using the keyboard, he types in Aeverless. The screen remains blank. He types in a few other cities he had visited, and the screen illuminates with past and information as current as five years ago on the screen. Still thinking that he was in the boundary of Oklahoma or Texas, he requested a full territory map. No mention of Aeverless appeared on either. Maybe he veered off course. He inquired to look at the boundary of Colorado, Arizona and New Mexico. Again, no mention of the town. It was very new or conveniently left off intentionally. Sensing he was not alone; he pauses and turns to see Brooks coming up behind him.

"Good morning," he smiles. She responds in like and takes a seat beside. A quick glance over, he discovers her attire and footwear are similar. This day, however, her hair is up in a messy ponytail bun. Something about her smell, the way she looks, pulls at his heartstrings. He knew distinctively that he would do anything to protect her from that moment on. He had to put her at ease quickly so they could work together.

"Did you enjoy your tour this morning," she asks sweetly, letting him know nothing goes unnoticed. "Listen," she starts, "I know it has an invasion on your privacy, but time and circumstances are not our friends here. I did something without asking your permission. Hear me about before you make a judgement. If you still disagree with me, I will render you unconscious and dump you back where I found you." She pauses for a moment to see if he has his undivided attention. Seeing that she does, he wonders just what happened this morning besides his snooping to her quickly, wanting to work together. From the tone of her last statement, it did not appear to be good news. She relays her tale about going to his vehicle and her sixth sense alarming. She motions for him to follow her. Going back through the atrium she stops at rather obese tree. Placing her hand on the tree, it opens to the security hub on this floor. She sits at one of chairs and motions him to do the same. Accessing the monitor, she shows him the footage from both from this morning and earlier when finding him in the woods. Observing him, he appears as puzzled as she did.

"What or who are they?" he asks. She shrugs "I do not know. They could be the Shadows that many referred to seeing around the time of the war", her answer filled with skepticism. She cannot mention the telepathic draw she had to him when finding him in the woods. Never had she felt so connected to anyone outside of her parents. Sensing his apprehension about the recent development, she asks. "You probably could have traveled another day or two before your car broke down. What made you speed up?"

Remarkable, he has only known her for less than a day and her intuitive mind is reading him like a book. He suspected it had more to do with the little prick he felt this morning. But even before then, it was as if he had known her all his life. "I think you call it sixth sense. I just had the feeling, the night before that I was being watched."

"About how long where you on the road the next morning before you broke down?"

"Maybe six or seven hours,"

"Have you seen or run across any undead that look like this," she asks.

He shakes his head before responding, "They don't look like or move like any undead I've seen. If these are the Shadows, they have morphed again into something new." They watch the Shadows a few minutes longer, ensuring that they captured decent images for future use. "We definitely need to develop something to detect them or we're doomed before we start."

Brooks quickly processes the information he has given her. "Listen, we must trust each other. We have no choice here. Argo has adjusted so you will monitor the security. For certain precautions, he has restricted certain things from us both for our safety if we get breached or must leave here. If either of us gets captured or severely injured, we cannot give the undead any vital information about this place. This morning I had him insert a data chip in both of us. For my benefit, I do not know where on your body it is, and I will not divulge where mine is located. This will allow us access to the system from a distance and telepathic access to each other." To show, she asks him to leave the room and go towards the elevator. Once he reaches it, he hears her in his ear to request access to the garage floor. He responds in silence that he will meet her there. Entering the elevator, he speaks aloud. "What floor is the garage on?"

"The eighth floor,"

"Eighth floor it is then." The door close and within seconds open to the eighth floor. He exits and looks to his left, right and straight ahead. The floor resembled a floor blown garage. There were several all-terrain vehicles, several jeeps, and a mid-size boat, a couple of tanks and one unique utility vehicle. A few seconds later, Brooks joins him at the entrance. "Come on, let's talk and walk," she motions. "There's a reason Aeverless doesn't appear in any almanac. The government purposely did not want anyone, especially foreign entities, knowing anything about the work they did here. They scattered records and documents through several databases and inquiries that provide bits and pieces. One would need to know exactly what to look for to paint a complete map." Pointing towards the utility vehicle she smiles "this is Hondo. My dad was an engineer and in his spare time he worked on making this baby immune to heat, cold and added extras in case we needed to live in the open. He died before finishing it, but I continued the redesign to streamline it. It is ready. We may have to put it to use. This vehicle can travel up to twelve hundred miles, barring no mechanical breakdowns that I have not come up with a scenario for. It will adapt to human commands and make any necessary adjustments, allowing us to sleep to get up to eat or bathroom breaks. It is basically a small house on wheels. The exterior is immune to acid, bullet and bomb proof. They reinforce the windows. There are security measurements that will allow us to lock and unlock remotely and start and move. Ready to learn? We will not start it today. I want you to look it over. Tell me if there's anything I missed."

"Wow," he nods, "you left nothing to chance. Thank you for being upfront with me. I want you to know that once I read or see something, I commit it to memory."

Entering Hondo, it surprises Alexander to see that she was right. Hondo resembled one of those old Boeing 737, only changed. They completely covered wheelbases like the base of Army tanks. The height of the vehicle was almost forty feet. The interior had a lab and medical area, a decontamination room, kitchen and living quarters and greenhouse. Brooks' father was quite a genius. He made this vehicle to be as immune, unbreakable, and undetectable as possible.

They spent the next several hours discussing every crook and section of Hondo, from the engines, to the undercarriage, every internal and external seam. He reviewed the fuel and water tanks, and addressed his concerns about food, medical supplies, how they would dispose of waste, how they would sterilize contaminated water or clothing; everything he felt was important to ensure they survived. After it satisfied him, they turn the discussion to the chip. The chip allowed them instant access to both Argo and Hondo, both telepathically and verbally. Any unwanted sound or noise above ground could cost you your life if you were not careful. The undead and the animals had an incredible hearing range. It was important that they left nothing to chance. They broke to eat and continued the conversation. They talked about everything from their childhood, to security to what they knew about the borders and territories that surrounded them. The more they conversed the stronger their bond grew, each knowing that they would know protect the other until the bitter end. For four days they watched the monitors, talked, studied history and worked on their exit plan. Neither had any plans or notions to venture outside or much less anywhere close to the garage or bank entrance to the facility. They did not even chance fully starting Hondo for fear the shadows would hear the sound. On the fifth day, they returned to the garage at midday and worked on the control board inside the vehicle.

"We left once and travelled to Abilene,"

"Abilene? Texas or Kansas?"

"Texas. It is about 350 miles from here. The old air base had spare parts and people living there. Come to discover, there is another underground facility there. According to the council here, the government built 15-20 unique facilities between their northern, southern, western and eastern borders. Each facility has its own unique fail safe. If we were to travel there, we have our own security codes and protocols that would give us access. It was another security measure put in place to secure the environment from the undead and the warring gangs." She pauses, becoming melancholy. "One procedure was to send a check in signal every week. I have not received one from at least ten locations in the past three months. I do not know what to think. Were they breached or was there some medical emergency that is preventing the response? The procedure was just a signal, no video or voice interactions. If we were to leave here, Abilene would be my recommended first stop."

"Do you know anything about the terrain and area? You're right, it's a possibility that might be worth the risk."

"Only what I remember as a child and it's hazy. There are no advantages. Abilene is flat, no mountains to speak off. We could be an easy target if spotted, and they still occupy the base. I suspect they probably put some security parameters in place at least five to ten miles in every direction. As dangerous as nightfall is, we would have to time it perfectly to arrive during the day and get to the bunker facility as soon as possible. There is an alcove in the library that stores some old maps. We can check them."

"Alexander, Brooks," Argo interrupts. "Come to control. There's something you need to see." Leaving the garage bay, they made their way to the main security hub. It seems their shadow in the woods had finally succumbed after five days of mist permeating the air and ground. His friends had not returned yet, but they knew it was a matter of time. They prayed that the shadow's skeletal remains would disintegrate, leaving no smell or trace. Remains would only make his buddies more determined to scout the area. No remains may give them the sense that maybe he moved on to follow his mysterious prey.

~

Later that evening, while stocking Hondo for possible travel, he inquires why everything was hard coded to the servers. He explained that in Chicagoland and many of the towns and cities he has visited, there were some printed material that still existed. He watched her in silence for a few moments, like was she trying to determine where to start her explanation.

"Remember, I started my story saying Aeverless is safe, but there was a heavy price to staying here. Once you arrived, you could not leave. It took years for my parents to gain their trust. My mother was a librarian. Education, especially history, was extremely important to her. They have sealed the section below us for over five years. Technology was not the only testing done here. Apparently in the mid-21st century, something landed here, alien. They captured it. Apparently, the spaceship or spacecraft was in pieces. The government housed several components in each of the underground facilities they were building. The discovered life form, found in the wreckage, ended up being stored here."

"What?" he exclaims.

"Yeah, what were they thinking is exactly what my parents said when they were finally privy to the information. I had just turned nine. We had been living in Aeverless since I was four years old. This is when they also were told about the other facilities. I think my parents stumbled into a situation where they finally had no choice but to tell them. They could not afford to lose an engineer of my dad's caliber. A librarian, yeah, for they saw her as just another schoolteacher. But my dad who had degrees in chemical and mechanical engineering. He was valuable. Anyway," removing the bitterness from her voice, "apparently each facility sent communications on the projects and conditions of the town and surrounding areas. As the undead spread and became more sophisticated, the verbal updates ceased, and they encrypted the information instead." She pauses and closes her eyes. He could tell from her tone she endured some pain and heartache over the events she had yet unfolded. After a few minutes, she opens her eyes and continues.

"One of the resident council members was a scientist and could clone something from the remains. I think I was around 13 or 14. He was becoming psychotic and with the weather being stable for a while, a lot of traffic was passing. One day a car broke down, like your situation and the occupants, a man and woman walked through the forest finding their way to the town. What we did not realize, someone or something infected the woman. They thought they had found some cure, which slowed changing. She in turns infects our resident scientist. All that time it gave them free rein to information, all of it. By the time, the changing started taking effect, it was too late. Out of two hundred people, only ten were unaffected. We closed the doors to the floor, sealed it, and acid bombed the hell out of it.

It took four days before all the screaming stopped. We decide that only one person would stay, and the rest would venture out in different directions to the remaining facilities, hoping to God that it would prevent the same mistake. I ended up staying here. The morning before my friends left, we burned every printed material we had. From that point on, if you did not know the code, you could not decipher the data to find the keys for information. That was two years ago," she whispered. She wipes her face, refusing the tears to fall.

"You mentioned that there were ten of you left. Were they close in age to you? Have you heard anything from them since?"

Clearing her throat, she nods. "Yes, only Brett and Ava, no one else. Brett made it to Abilene and Ava to Baylift. The communication stopped two months ago. For months after they left, I was fearful of being infected too. I always had Argo as a personal handheld since I was a little girl. My dad built it before we left New York for him to be a travelling guide, play friend for me. As I aged, he tweaked the program but never built him. It must have been some sixth sense of his. He would always tell me the plans of his design, but never show them to me. After a couple of months here by myself, I realized I was going to need some help. I set down at the monitors to draw out the design. My dad had left me some breadcrumbs as the file of the design was on the server. Until you showed up, Argo and the other two AIs have been my companions for the last eighteen months.”

“Please don’t misconstrue my next comments. I mean no harm. The aim is to help strategize and give us some advantages, okay,” he implores. She nods her willingness to listen. “I’m going to start at the two-year mark and work backwards. After your friends left, were any new security programs and protocols put in place?”

“Yes, when no one returned within two months, I scrubbed all the old protocol and security programs and installed new ones. I sealed all but four entry ways into the facility.”

“Good,” he interrupts. “Hold that information for a minute. You mentioned after they sealed the infected floors, it took four days for the infected to die. By chance is there any footage of it. I have been working with Argo on creating images of the undead I have seen. It will give us a sign if there are different variations through inbreeding with animals or something else.”

“Yes. I have never seen the footage, but I have breadcrumbs on how to pull it up. Let us call it quits here for now and head back to the library.” He agrees. They secure the garage floor and make their way back to the library security hub. From conversations she learned Alexander was the son of a police detective and his mother was a surgeon. He too had grown up going to the best schools. They left Chicagoland when he was twelve years old. Not only did he commit to memory every book he read, but he was a remarkable reader of people. Like her parents, he taught him everything valuable about their professions. He was a natural born leader, so he took charge often.

Booting up the database, she enters a series of numbers and words. "What timeframe do you want to see," she asks. "Let's look at the last two months before you sealed the floors." Nodding, she types in another few commands. After several minutes, the system uploads the video from a few years ago. "Listen, anytime you want to stop, let me know okay. We can watch this over a period of days, a little at a time. We're looking for anything helpful we can use." In unison, they repeat, "knowledge is power." The video begins in silence, just as movies were when they were first created early in the 20th century. Seeing the entire town on camera, the entries plus the entire underground facility, he realized that the facility was three times larger than the town. It surprised even Brooks, which triggered a memory about the hidden alcove in the library. Inside there several old maps.

"I almost forgot. There is an alcove area in the library that has some old maps there. Do you think they might be of help?"

Alexander's eyes light up. "Yes, it does. After we finish reviewing this, I would like to see it. Is there a way we can scan the maps somehow, make them a part of our new database? It would be helpful in our travels." She agrees and resumes explaining the underground areas on the screen. He asks her to pause of a minute. "This area here," pointing to a shaded grey area off of the main cafeteria, "can we get to it?"

"Yes, I've never ventured there, but yes, we can make it operational in a couple of days."

"Let us do that. It gives us another option way out and will buy us some more time here if needed. First thing tomorrow, let us get started with it. You can hit resume now." For the next few hours, they watch the video, making notes to each other and committing the entire layout of the underground to memory. They stop for a brief rest and agree to meet in the common kitchen area in a few hours.

~

For the next month, with Argo's help, they prepped the new area for occupancy as they continued their vigilance in monitoring the external cameras and scouring the old footage for clues about the infection. They changed their diet to include more protein and vitamins so their body would adjust to the outdoor climate. As much natural lighting as they created in the facility, it was no match for the actual world. All the preparations in the world would go to waste if they could not adjust to the climate.

They dismantled the other two AIs and use their parts for security sweeps; drones that can move through the terrain before them. Each had a travel distance of up to five hundred miles before they disintegrate. As neither had no clue about what laid before them, the drones would help find shelter and detecting any unknown bobby traps. They spent the first two days opening the vents and fumigating the entire space. After quarantining it for another three days, they ventured into the space in complete protective gear. The additional space, dub by them as New Beginning, was two floors which encompassed twelve thousand feet. They designed the first floor to have a loft area as living quarters and space for a medical lab, a workspace as the data and security center, a quarantine area and a greenhouse. The second floor housed Hondo and the exit to a tunnel area leading out of town. Each day they work for twelve hours, six getting New Beginnings ready, and the other six reviewing the external security footage, the old film and creating new protocols and security programs, readying themselves for the day they would need to move from Aeverless. Each day they worked, knowing that they could not let up. When the time came, they would be ready to move.

Day 48 started with a change in the routine. Since all the inventory and equipment needed, except a lone server was now in New Beginning, they began closing vents and sealing all the floors except for the third, which gave them direct access to their new home. Alexander redirected the security hub to the living quarters and from there they would run the program to destroy it, the medical lab, and garage and quarantine area within two hours too. The outside paradise and greenhouse were already closed for over three days. Today they were dismantling the last items they would take with them from the third floor when the security monitor registered two alarms, both occurring within a three-hour time span. The first was the old footage capturing the last images of the infected on the third day before the space went silent. The transformation had completed, and the infected bore any eerie resemblance to the shadows that had attempted to follow Brooks back to Aeverless.

"Oh my God," she exclaimed. "If, no, when they return, they won't leave until they find this place and a way in."

"Agreed, I think our best bet now is to put as much distance between us and them as soon as possible. Our last defense will provide us with eyes and ears. We will need to sense their presence and how to stay ahead of them." They had just stared working on updates to Hondo, from the third-floor server, when the second alarm chimes. Dust had settled and nightfall had just begun its descent. In the area where the lone shadow had made camp, six shadows appeared. Alexander, on watch, pressed the intercom and asked Brooks to join him. For a few moments they watched as two stayed and the other four ventured out in different directions. Looking at each other, they nod. "It's time, Brooks," he whispers. "Argo, we're on our way to you. Our friends have returned. Start the countdown. If your friends encountered this breed, we need to rethink some strategies as they may be more intelligent than we think. We have to work with the possibility of they may know how to get inside."

Grabbing the server and the last items they collected, they load them onto their carts and make their way back to the common area, shutting down everything in their path. At the refrigerated area both enter the security codes, which opens to a long narrow pathway. They follow the path until reaching another similar door. Again, they enter the security codes and walk through three more doors before entering the loft area of New Beginning. At the security monitor, they witness acid mist destroying the rest of the floors that had been Brooks' home for over two years. Entering a last series of codes, she seals the space. With the new protocol activated, the screen lightens, and her father appears in front of an empty backdrop.

"Brooks, if you have activated this program, it must mean you have to leave Aeverless. In this file is the name and locations of all twelve facilities, twenty safe underground shelters plus another that I have discovered outside of the northern territory. It is in the country once called Guatemala. I have programmed the coordinates of how to get there for you. I have also programmed some other details that will pop up as you need them. As this program was for you only, do not share your security knowledge, the programs or protocols with anyone from this facility. It is no longer safe. Everything will make sense as you see it. Hopefully, these will help you make your way to Guatemala. Good luck and Godspeed. I love you."

She remains still for several moments, shell-shocked at the message her father left. Alexander touches her shoulder, jarring her back to the present. "You must have had some internal awareness Brooks for you to make the changes you did. Your father trusted this and gave you, us an exit strategy. Do not beat yourself up. Your father would be proud of you and I'm grateful."

"Thanks. There something about you I trust. I'm glad I have you and Argo," she responds. "Now it's a race to get out of here alive and stay as far ahead of these things as we can. I am excited, but I am scared shitless."

"Me too, but I trust you. I trust Argo. We are going to give this everything we got. First sign of daylight, we move out Brooks. Agreed?" he implores. Argo answers for her "yes, first sign of daylight. I have security watch tonight. You guys sleep."

"Thanks, Argo," Brooks replies. "Can you set the new coordinates for the safe houses with the facilities? It would interest to see if they are halfway points, which gets us off the grid and throws our pursuers off track." They leave Argo and take the last items from the facility down to Hondo, where they will spend their last night in Aeverless.

Settling down, both remarks on how the Intel on Guatemala was accurate. They guessed that the tunnel before would give them cover for maybe a day. Once they exit, they would destroy it, leaving no way to return to Aeverless. With the additional information about the twenty underground safe houses, they become a little more optimistic about their journey and hopes for Guatemala.

~

Dawn came much earlier than they expected. With Argo now on board after transferring the latest video footage of the night, they open the bay doors and exit New Beginning. With Hondo being forty feet in height, she glided through the tunnel with ease, making them aware that the tunnel had to at least span fifty feet in height, with less than three feet on each side of the vehicle as passable space. After crossing the fourth security bay door, Brooks shuts down the power grid and begins the denotation sequence for two hours later, forever barring them from entering the underground facility. Following her father's coordinates, at the two hours mark they had already travelled through four different tunnel paths. The town council, and generations before them, took great pains to develop the underground tunnels. Nothing grew or lived, just a dark place. There was no humidity in the air and the temperature read a cool 48 degrees. To err on the safe side, they always kept their protective gear on. Hondo was spraying mist behind them, covering the trail, leaving no clues that something had disturbed it. The lights on Hondo were infrared and tailored to adjust to any lighting situation. The glow from the lights adjusted to the tunnel as not to disturb any unknowns. It provided a full 360-degree view for a full two hundred feet ahead. Some sections of the walls had pictured carvings on them. They recorded the scenes, hoping the database could decipher the drawings, language and century. It would help them estimate their location on the old maps, which they scanned at the library before destroying. Once above ground, they could reset the lights to adjust to the conditions plus scan up to 450 yards ahead of them. They decided each would take an eight-hour shift navigating through the tunnels. Two days later they neared their first major crossing, a bridge which seem to span for about a mile or more. As on cue, her dad's voice vibrates through the speakers.

"Before you cross the bridge, first turn off your database and electronics. Do not turn it back on until after you have crossed the bridge. The distance across is two miles and there is some electrical current going on. Second, once you cross the bridge it is imperative that you destroy it on your side. Whatever you can do to disable or impede someone or something from progressing, do it. At the end of the bridge are five pathways. The first will face you. Last, turn your database and electronics back on and take the second tunnel on your right. The coordinates I have set will resume. From that point, if traveling in vehicle you will have another twelve to sixteen hours before you reach the last exit. If you have reached this point close to nightfall, I recommend waiting here until morning. You'll understand."

Listening to her father's advice, they decide to make camp here and begin again one hour after full dawn break. So far nothing registered on the security devices above ground that the perimeters were in jeopardy. From the last security door at New Beginning, it took them a full two days to get to this point. Twenty four-hour head start was great, but the more distance and time they can put between them and the shadows the better.

At dawn they disabled the electronics and begin the trek across the bridge. The silence was more deafening than the tunnels they had just exited, sending a chill through both Alexander and Brooks. To make matters worse, there was this weird glow in the fog that lit their path across the bridge. On instinct it was as if Hondo had a life of its own, as it made its way across, lights illuminating their way, pointing straight ahead, not veering in any other direction but north. The thirty-five-minute trek seemed more like two hours as they moved at a snail's pace. Reaching ground on the other side, they spot low illuminating lights in each of the five tunnels. They move ahead twenty feet and discharge detonators that will explode fifteen minutes after entering the tunnel path her father recommended. Entering the tunnel, they turn all the electronics back on and Hondo, again on instinct, picks up speed and heads toward their unknown. The detonators exploded, sending tremors through the tunnels. No one would get suspicious as tremors often rocked the area. The occurrences became normal for this area after the massive storm twenty years ago. Looking in the rear-view mirror they see the pathway is no longer useable, large rocks and concrete foundation spread from the floor of the tunnel to the ceiling. They resume their gaze forward and continue the path before them. The temperature gauge rises from 48 to 65 within a three-hour period and then again to 80 in another ninety minutes. At the six hours mark, with tunnel temperature reaching 150 degrees, they spot another bay door 50 yard ahead. When they get within twenty-five feet, the server illuminates a series of codes. Her father's voice returns and gives directions on how to open the bay door without leaving the vehicle and how to access the bay door if they were on foot. From the bridge to this marker, it had taken them another fourteen hours. In the morning, they would leave Aeverless forever. At dawn, following the directions, they open the gated doors and exited Aeverless. The door closes behind them, and they watch on the monitor as the handles and locks disintegrates within seconds. She jokes out loud, "so much for returning. Looks like the exit codes were for one use only."

Annotating their travel time in the database, they activate the interactive map of the external world. To their surprise, they discovered they were still in the territory called New Mexico. The tunnels took them back under Aeverless in the opposite direction of Abilene, with west leading them into the old territory called Arizona, north keeping them in New Mexico, and south bordering the territory of old Texas and Mexico. Puzzled, her father's voice again chimes with an explanation. The town council had realized the additional strain of undead. This group was intelligent and had been collecting information as they roamed from town to town. "Apparently," he continues, "one of the shadow leaders infected a scientist at the facility called Noah's Ark. Their quest to find a cure before becoming infected went in vain, but the knowledge carried and traveled, becoming a conglomerate with each fresh addition. Knowing that people from Aeverless made a trip to Abilene, that would be the first place they would suspect you would run to. I have inputted the coordinates for a safe house located another four hours from here. It has been uninhibited and will allow you a few weeks to lie low, gather whatever supplies are there, and input your security protocols and programs. There is a deposit of information there that should be helpful. I'll provide you the keys once you get close."

Hondo makes the adjustments inside and to the windows that see out but cannot make out anything in the interiors and to the wheels to prevent melting. The coordinates read south. "South it is to a destination four hours ahead," Alexander chimes in, his voice steady to provide the positivity they need. They dispatch the first drone ahead and make their way through the trail for another twenty miles before coming upon a highway. With the drone showing a clear path ahead for another fifty miles, the vehicle sets a cruising speed and makes its way to the safe house in the mountains of Quitman.

Deep in the canyon below the bridge, the tremors continued to rumble as the ground shifted and cracked, exposing a silver oblong shaped looking canister. A strange eerie taping replaced the tremors until the shape broke open. From the crevices, a thick black ooze seeped out and made its way up the canyon wall. Reaching the remaining tunnels, it stretched itself to human form and investigated the surrounding ground. Mimicking a centipede, several arms canvassed the mouth of each tunnel, returning particles to the base of the ooze. After several minutes, two lone arms detach themselves after finding a miniscule opening at the tunnel Brooks and Alexander traveled through and followed. The remaining of the ooze returned to the human base and dissolved into the ground, waiting for orders to follow or for the arms to return.

~

Brooks takes in all in. She had not been outside for more than a couple hours at a time since the trip her family had taken to Abilene when she was thirteen.

According to the almanac, it was the start of spring and they had assigned her family to stay at the facility until September. Reflecting on her memories now, she did not understand why they returned around two months later. She noticed, however, the change in her parents. In the company of the town council, they were active, just as they had always been. In their living space, they limited the conversations. Her parents insisted they talk in code, and it was imperative that those conversations stayed within their quarters. Riding down the road now, looking at the open highway, she shared this story with Alexander. One thing about him, he always listened first and kept an open mind. Before he spoke, he always summed up the conversation, when she was reliving her experiences with her parents and the people of Aeverless. She guessed his father had honed that trait. Listen, gather the facts, ensure you heard them and then make your observations. As usual, he waited a few minutes before responding. "I'm assuming now that you see some parallel you didn't see before that something happened at Abilene to make your parents become cautious," he began. "We don't know if your Dad will send us to Abilene or share some insight into why he elected for us to go to the safe house in Quitman first. We may never know. It might be information he thinks may be detrimental to our survival. What we know, there is more to Aeverless and these other government facilities than they led us to believe on the surface. Maybe your father uncovered what their actual mission or purpose was and is letting the story unfold as we travel, allowing us to work through his assessment. Let us see what happens once we get there. He had his reasons for directing us there first. We'll reevaluate once we get there."

She nods in agreement, as he knew she would. She had already come to that conclusion. He liked that she always bounced her thoughts to him. To ensure she was on the right path, and now because they were companions. They have each other. Traveling and living alone gets lonely and depressing. He did not know how she survived alone if she did. But then again, she had Argo. It is something about human interaction that you cannot beat. They continued the highway with nothing in sight but road. The terrain was desolate, nothing but road, gravel and heat. The temperature gauge peaked at 165 degrees. Hondo showed no signs of malfunction, and it was quite comfortable inside. They attempted to create some different scenarios based on the information they gained.

In reviewing the history on each of the twenty facilities, four areas are on or near a military facility. They knew about Abilene, which had underground bunkers and was once home to what history described as an Air Base with aircraft carriers, jets, bombers and planes. It looks as though the government was intent on the general population not knowing about these facilities. They were two other facilities that her father mentions in passing, one in the state called Arizona and the other in the state called Utah. About 100 miles from their destination, they passed some skeletal remains on the road. It appeared to be some type of animal. Not stopping or slowing, the cameras recorded the scene and continued onward. Another ten miles passed before the drone sent the last report. With the way clear, they entered the final coordinates to the safe house.

What her father had estimated to be four hours, took them just shy of the three-hour mark. Following the mountain trail, they reach the marker marking the entrance of the safe house. They screened the trees for signs of life and the shadows. There were nonvisible. At the marker, her father gives her the directions for access. Argo and Alexander exit the vehicle and walk one hundred feet to the deserted ranger station. After sweeping the perimeter and interior, they make their way to utility cabinet in the far-right-hand corner. At some point they had rifled it through, but untouched. Argo extends his hand through the third shelf and finds the hidden keypad. Placing his hand on top it illuminates. From Hondo, Brooks informs them that just another couple of feet ahead of them a lift rises from the ground. Retracing their steps back to the vehicle, Alexander and Argo join Brooks at the control panel and they make their way forward and park on it. The lift was quite round in diameter, large enough to hold a full-size plane that weighed several tons. After what appeared to be a radar scan of the vehicle which recorded every internal image, the lift descends. They ride in silence for about another twenty minutes. The lift, moving at a steady pace, comes to a stop about thirty miles underground to a bay door built about fifty feet in height. It opens and they drive inside, with the lift returning to the surface and the door closing behind them.

Adjusting the lights, they send a security drone ahead. The screen on the panel pulls up a map of the interior. This was an airport hangar, changed with several amenities, built by the government after the war in 2096. The accommodations are first class, as it was to be a safe house for the highest officials in the land, after they destroyed four locations through an act of terrorism. The drone completed its sweep of the facility in fifty minutes. They estimated that the sun was just beginning its slumber for the day. Good news was they had made it to the coordinates and were at least safe from the outside elements.

As the audio continued providing the backdrop of their destination, we activated other programs to provide full power to the facility. Her father explains they built the facility in 2113 using covert military funds. They stored the complete plans for this location and other two he mentioned at Aeverless. The strategy was, after destruction of the previous locations, the government wanted only two facilities on land, two on the oceans and one in space that would house the top government officials. They came up with a random program if activated would send the designated members, along with a handful of qualified personnel from each industry, health, education and environmental to those locations. None would know which facility they were being sent to until a genuine emergency warranted it. Quarterly they would continue with emergency drills that would prepare them and keep them ready in an event.

After they gave the all clear, they proceeded ahead another half a mile and parked. Upon passing a hidden sensor, another bay door closes behind them. They adjust the lighting to give them a full view of their new home for the next few weeks, an underground oasis far from the likes of Aeverless. Still driving Hondo, they notice a street path. It is circular with four buildings each connected by what appeared to be a floating crosswalk three floors up, at its center. The first building appeared to have five floors, but then two buildings were about 12 floors high, with the last building being only three floors. Her father explains that the one with three floors is the garage where they can park Hondo. The two tallest buildings were living quarters, with the remaining housing a full medical wing, sports complex and greenhouses. Each of the living quarters had medical and security kiosks with underground access back to the garage in case of an overhead breach. They enter at the entrance and park. Although the drone had cleared the area, not detecting any anomalies, they decide they will spend the first night in Hondo. If nothing made a surprise visit during the night, they would venture out to tour the buildings the next morning. After running maintenance checks and completing some minor security measures, they take a break to eat. Thinking out loud, she wonders how her father knew so much about the security protocols and programs for covert military operations. "You don't think he stumbled across either, do you," she asks turning her full attention to Alexander.

"No, I don't," he responds. "Although my dad spoke about many people believing in the conspiracy theories after the war in 2096. The world went through an environmental crisis in 2092. Half of the world's water resources became contaminated, killing thousands of people, animals and vegetation. At the start of 2096, information leaked that certain countries in Europe had developed and disseminated the virus in hope to clear the world of what they considered being a sub-par society. Riots began, terrorism grew, and the war stemmed from people fighting against this new line of socialism coming to life. More and more government policies on security became covert operations and facilities. There was no proof of it, just theories. Your dad discovered they were true."

"Hm," her head shaking, "it's possible, but I think there's more to it," she starts while strumming her fingers on the table in front of her. "There was a phrase he repeated from a song he loved. Every day, during the day, he would repeat it. At the time it made little sense to me, but now with what we have learned so far, I think everything my father did had an agenda to it." Returning to the control panel she typed lines from a childhood story her father used to read to her. The screen goes black for a few seconds and a video appears. She calls for Alexander and Argo.

They meet her at the control and see she is staring at the image in front of them. "It's my father," she says out loud. Sensing her anxiety, Alexander sits beside her. He takes her hands, thus breaking her concentration from the screen. "We've had a very eventful day. For the first time in over two years, you have been outside for over two hours. Not only that, but you have also left the only home you have ever known. Brooks," he hesitates. "Brooks, please, look at me. Let us step back for a minute to breathe. We have learned a lot today. Let us get a couple hours of rest, tour the buildings. While we do that, Argo is going to complete the rest of the security sweeps and place the remaining sensors online." Alexander stops, knowing that anything spoken after this point would not register. He could see how strong she was trying to remain, but everything about the day and now the last few hours were taking a toll. He leaves the console area and beckons Argo to follow him. Making his way to the living quarters, he packs a few items.

"Argo."

"Yes, Zander." Zander became a code word between the AI and Alexander when during security details. Alexander hated the slang and ignored Argo when he used it. This last instance, however, the tone was pointed, almost as if the AI was riling him up. Getting back to Argo, he inquires which floor in the second and third building had the best advantage points. Argo confirms that it also connected the seventh floor between the two tallest buildings. He recommended that floor. "If we were to take some downtime, me and Brooks," he asks, "how much time can we afford right now. Your best guess." Argo says that he can handle things for at least a week, but to err on the side of caution, two days may be just what she needs. Alex nods, thanking him. "I'm going to get Brooks. Grab our portable server so we can link into the security hub and finish the encryption link between here and our new residence. I'll meet you there in about thirty minutes." He returns to the console for Brooks. She has not moved an inch; her body numb from the image on the screen.

"We have to go, Brooks," he implores. She turns to him. Her eyes watery. At that moment she seemed so small and defeated. "Brooks," he shouts, "move, now." Hoisting her by her arm, he leads her from the vehicle. Securing it behind them, they exit the garage. The first thing that they discover is that it is well lit. Looking upward, it appeared to be a sky with stars. The temperature reading on their monitor displayed 72 degrees. It was quite comfortable indeed. They made their way down the sidewalk, noticing the real evergreens and other plants. For aesthetics, the place gave a sense of home and not some sterile environment. Depending upon how long the crisis was for, the designers and engineers took great care to make it as inviting as possible. Leaving the garage, the entrance to the third building took about 15 minutes. They could see no lights or anything to determine what the interior holds. The same was true of the garage. Until one entered, the outside gave no visible appearance of what was inside or signs of life. The entrance of the third building, there appeared to be a scan and keycard on both sides of the entrance. As they approached, the doors opened. Argo informed them he had already scanned their vitals and the doors would open for them. For security measures, he was creating special keys for manual access. Taking Brooks by the hand, Alexander escorts her inside.

The lobby atrium was bright, filled with a rainbow of flowers and shrubbery. For as far as they could see in every direction, the structure, reinforced plexiglass, was breathable, open yet allowed discretion where needed. Turning to face the outside, they could see the street, sidewalk and trees. They make their way to the freestanding elevator platform and it glides upwards toward the seventh floor. From first glance, the bones of the building showed no signs of walls or wiring from previous generations of structures. The foundation was impressive. Upon reaching the designated floor, the platform moves inward to the center of the space. They step onto the walkway and the bones change from transparent to solid mass. On the wall, to their right, is an interactive floor plan describing the layout. Argo meets them in the hall in between their apartments.

"Here are your manual key cards," Argo explains as he hands them each a small black placard. He opens the door of each apartment. Alexander thanks him as Brooks remains quiet. Since leaving the garage, her eyes have taken in all the scenery, but she remained silent. Argo frowns in frustration, not knowing what to say or do to help his friend. He looks at Alexander, puzzled. Placing his hand on his friend Alex responds, "Let me handle this for a while my friend. She will be okay. I promise." Argo give a thumbs up and states he is heading for the principal building to complete the rest of the security installations. He mentions that there are monitors that access any utility, camera of the entire facility, even the hidden sensors leading in and out of the area in a fifty-mile radius. "So as soon as we triggered the first one, we were on the facility's radar," Alexander asks. Argo confirms his question and informs him that somehow it did not trigger us as a threat. "It knew we were coming," Brooks speaking for the first time since leaving the garage. Looking Alexander dead in the eyes she continues, "You believe me now don't you. There's no way my dad accidently found out all of this knowledge." The pure thought of it angered her. Her entire life she believed her dad was just a structural engineer who worked on buildings for the commonwealth of New York. Alexander motions for Argo to complete his assignment.

"Listen to me, Brooks. I do not doubt you at all. But jumping to conclusions is not the thing that has kept us alive. Facts, truths have sustained us. Your father has given us many road maps. Let us listen to him and get the facts. Once we have them, then we'll make some sound decisions." They enter the apartment. The ambience is warm, and lavender filled the air. Leading her to the bedroom, he asks her to sit on the bed. He enters the bathing area and starts the water. Returning to her, he tells her to take a shower and leaves the room before returning to the kitchen area. Finding the panel, he orders two cups of tea and a small bottle of brandy. Retrieving them, he makes his way to the seating area and waits for Brooks. Several minutes go by and Alexander is still waiting. Hearing the water still running, he goes into the bedroom. No Brooks. He taps on the door to the bathing area and does not get a response. Entering the area, he sees her shadow sitting on the shower floor. Without hesitation, he joins her there and takes her into his arms. Turning off the water, he towels her off and helps her dress. The evidence of the exhaustion and tears cried showed on her face, her eyes puffy and red. Placing her on the bed, she curls up into herself. At that moment all he wanted to do was lie next to her, but he knew she was not quite ready to take that next step yet. Instead, he lies on the floor beside the bed. After a time, she falls asleep. Alexander then closes his eyes and does the same.

The Past

The Fathers–Year 2237

Worthington Coveia was not a man to engage in small chatter. Feigning sleep, he closed his eyes to keep his seat companion from further drawing him into idle conversation. Over six feet tall, with Scandinavian good looks and a slim muscular build, Worth, as they knew him among his college friends and professors, excelled in everything he set his mind to. An academic and athletic scholarship landed him at the most prestige school where he could graduate with degrees in biochemistry, astrophysics and electrical engineering in less than five years. Many think he would have continued to play sports, but an early injury during his first year made Worth realign his timetable along with his goals. His drive and passion for both chemistry and engineering peaked attention of the new government. He accepted their offer to serve as a bio-specialist with the Guardians, a covert agency designed to safeguard New America's infrastructure, at the end of his college experience.

Part of his training required Worth to attend combat and special ops training. Every summer before graduating he spent a grueling ten weeks learning and absorbing every physical and mental endurance test and training they threw at him. He never complained. For him, complaining or worrying was negative energy he just did not have time for. His parents were whiners until Worthington was born. Upon his birth they saw him as a golden meal ticket. Born as Brooks Oliver Johansson, his family paraded him in front of every entertainment scout and film director. He made them a good living until the untimely death of his mother and sister. They had accompanied him to an audition when a speeding driver ran through the intersection, hitting their car and killing his mother and sister instantly. His father, blaming Brooks for their death, never recouped, becoming a bitter and angry alcoholic who blew their settlement money in less than two years. Brooks at ten years of age knew then that he could only rely on himself. Years later with several college offers in hand he caught transportation out of New Region Florida, enrolled in school, changed his name and never looked back. Now with graduation less than a month in his rear-view window, he is on a shuttle hover on his way to his first station assignment, Quitman Mountains, in the middle of nowhere region called Texas.

After a few moments, the seat companion in obvious need of a listener moved, allowing him to reopen his eyes and view the landscape before him. There was quite a difference between the terrain of Old Canada, New York, to what elders knew as Louisiana and Texas. The shuttle stops in Dallas Land, where Worth picks up the motor craft that was left for him at the station. He had another eight hours of travel as his superiors wanted him to leave no trace of his travels or existence from this point forward. First stop is Abilene, where after grabbing a quick bite to eat, he picks up some more luggage that was left for him at the old train station. He resumes and makes it to the edge of Quitman by nightfall. At first glance of the motorbike, he wondered why they chose this means of transportation, but upon arriving at Quitman he understood. Retrieving his night googles from his bag and map, he studies it while listening to the ground and sounds around him. Hearing no imminent threat, he returns the map to its pouch and makes way through the trail until coming upon the old ranger station. He parks the bike and makes his way inside. He walks to the coordinates given to him and finds the hidden keypad on the third shelf of the utility room. Placing his hand on top, he feels the ground shift beneath him. He exits the building and gets back on the motorbike. Moving it several feet ahead of him, he drives onto the circular lift, which then descends back into the earth.

Several minutes pass before the lift comes to a complete stop in front of two huge hangar doors. Within seconds the doors open, and he drives through. He passes through several more hangar doors until he reaches a sole street with four buildings. It connects two of the four, the third looks to have four floors, and the remaining is a single floor building. He drives up to the single floor building and enters. The inside of the building houses a large garage, complete with working bays. He spots four more motorbikes and parks his next in line. Grabbing just his small bag and backpack, he heads out towards the solo building with four floors. If one did not know any better, they would swear they were outside inside of over forty feet below ground. The ambience and interior of this portion of the hangar looked like an oasis.

He approaches the building, enters his credentials at the security kiosk. The doors open, letting him inside. Not taking time to observe the lobby or décor, he heads for the elevator and requests the second floor. When the door chimes open, he exits and heads for the first open door. Upon entering, four gentlemen look up from the table and rise to their feet.

The first, a black guy, with his same height and stature approaches him, hand out. "Hi, I'm Hennessey Whitehouse." The others approach and introduce themselves. Two of the guys were a good four inches taller than him, making them close to 6'7 or 6'8. The last was much smaller, but outweighed him by at least sixty pounds. For a heavy guy, he moved with the quickness and grace of a jaguar. It was also apparent that he was their lead, as he took charge of the meeting.

"Good afternoon, gentlemen. Sitting at this table is our core unit minus one. For the next two years, this is our home of operation. In front of your panels are your security codes, keys and dossier on each team member. Do not share your security credentials. After you have reviewed, commit to memory and then take the items to your designated burn spot. After today, we will no longer use our given names but will have an identifier only known to the six of us. If we were ever to go live in an active situation, these identifiers will become our lifelines. After you leave this facility and return to the outside world, should you have a family incorporate this identifier into your daily life as inconspicuous as possible? It is a lifeline for them as well. Teach them parts of our craft as a routine but not obvious to onlookers. We are this generation's gatekeepers and if wounded or we meet with death, it is our responsibility to ensure our family picks up that torch. Understood, questions," he pauses. Seeing none, he shakes his head in agreement. "Let's get to work."

After reviewing his files, he drops his gear off in building two. They all agree to meet at the dining floor at the end of the hour for dinner. They noticed they had one common like–porterhouse steaks. Out of that respect, they named their new home Porterhouse. Each talked about their background, leaving no detail, no matter how painful or embarrassing out. The primary aim was before their tenure was over, they needed to be brothers in every sense of the word. Their lives and humanity depended upon it. They even gave each one of the building a name that reflected their identifier. Central City referred to their team leader. Coral House and Gable Bay, referred to as Hulk 1 and Hulk 2, were first cousins. Whitehouse became Compton Corners, as he grew up in Compton. Until the latter part of the 21st century, they knew the city of Compton as a hard, mean place to grow up in. The tide changed with several persons returning and changing the community from crime ridden to one of the more premiere urban cities thriving from technology and education. Worth's handle became Daytona Boulevard, from his hometown in Florida and his hobby of tinkering with vehicles.

They filled each day with training sessions on everything from security to environmental. The crew became tight knit and after six months it was like they had known each other all their lives. Month seven, they turned their lives upside down as the last member of the team arrived. Their day started at dawn and ended around fifteen hours later. Each member was working on the security detail when an alarm alerted inside the perimeter. Central stayed at the hub while the remaining team spread out on patrol. From the outside, there was only one road that led to the main entrance of Quitman Mountains. One could enter through many trails, but without a map, it would be hard to find shelter or the other three ranger stations. They had wired every ranger station with security monitors that canvassed a five-mile radius in every direction. However, security did not detect a breach. Whatever or whoever they had already made down the lift, past the hangar doors and was inside the compound.

From their screens, they could see the image making its way to Central City. The group made their way to the coordinates to intersect. Each arrives on the second floor and forms a circular barrier at an anonymous-looking wall. From the command center, Central stood steadfast, fingers at the control, ready to activate barriers to exist to prevent the intruder from running rogue. Each waited with bated breath, frozen at the unknown. The wall opens and a lone woman walks out with hands up, assuming a neutral position. With Central standing barefoot at 5'7, she was shorter than maybe 5 feet. With scanner in hand, Worth moves closer, recording each vital and the skeletal structure of the woman. Whoever built her was more than good, they were excellent. Before them stood the latest artificial intelligence human to date. Despite the size in stature, she could handle and performing any function required of her, just as her counterparts.

 Predetermined before her arrival, only her designated handler would be privy to her information. They were not aware that an AI, much less designed as a woman, would be the latest to join their group; only that someone who would be the interface between them once they left the mountains. She would be the only one receiving and passing information. She was the repository. No one would know where her archive would land. For the next year they worked side by side, and solo creating possible crisis scenarios and solutions from droughts to acts of war. Relocation of critical personnel could happen within less than eight hours' notice, emergency personnel and crews needed to be ready to move and implement recovery protocols.

As they had named everything else at Quitman, they each chose their personal name as it was their key to the hidden dome, they named the Unknown. The Unknown led to a hidden exit and entrance to the outside world from the facility. Outside of being the repository and their contact after leaving Porterhouse, the girl's sole responsibility was building a vehicle or vehicles large enough to house over 100 people for a duration of over five years. The vehicle had to not only travel across dense terrain but also under several hundred feet of water if needed. The ability to travel at stealth mode, appear invisible and cover its movement were absolute necessities. If the enemy could penetrate the facility, the ability for them to follow needed to be a major factor.

A good size convoy capable of housing several types of metal structures and technology was quite the challenge. It needed to be high enough to travel through the dome's underground tunnels up to three hundred miles in every direction possible. During their time at Porterhouse, each team member traveled through the tunnels identifying strengths and weak points. They worked, individually and as a group, to redesign the weak points until satisfied it would be attack proof. From the tunnels there were ten exits, that without a map it would be impossible to find one's way back to the facility once they exited. As with each scenario laid out, every design created, once they perfected it, each man committed it to memory and destroyed all written documentation. Only the girl and encrypted clues in the database would lead another team to the vital information if needed. As Worth had a love of tinkering with all vehicles outside of his time here at Porterhouse, they had selected him as the girl's sponsor. His name for her was Bayja. It was also a bread crumb he would provide his family in the event they needed the key to get here and his next tour destination of Jalapa Guatemala before returning to New Region New York.

The Present

Brooks turns and checks the time. She slept for a whole six hours, a first for her. Sleep was four hours and maybe two thirty-minute catnaps during the day. She sees Alexander had not left her side. He was beside her on the floor. She watches his face, a serene peace about him. Eyes still closed; he asks if she is okay. "Why did you stay," she whispers. Opening his eyes, he studies her face. The puffiness gone, she still looked tired. "I stayed because you needed me," sitting up to get a better view and to calm the butterflies in his stomach. He stands and makes his way to the bathroom. After a few moments, he returns. "I'm going to check out my quarters. Breakfast in about twenty minutes?"

"Sure," she responds. Last night she barely noticed anything. She gazes around the room, checks out the bathing area and then heads to the main sitting and kitchen area. The space is quite large and comfortable. She notices that there is a large picture window and moves towards it. The mass turns to glass and gives the most amazing view to the atrium below. Noticing what appeared to be a closet door off the sitting area, she opens only to find it is a connecting door to Alexander's apartment. She retreats to her space and readies herself for the day ahead. While waiting for Alexander, she checks in with Argo. A secure link to Hondo from their new command center established, and all new security programs and protocols were in place. Now it was just a matter of them touring and memorizing each inch of their new home. Twenty minutes later, she opens her main door to Alexander's knock.

"We have a connecting door," she points to the door to the right in the living space.

"Good to know," he states. Sitting at the table, he grabs a piece of fruit that she has ordered for their meal. "Ready to talk about last night." He turns to watch her emotions. Much better. "It was just weird to see him on the screen, a much younger version of the man I remember," she starts. "We've just learned too much information for him to just stumble across, don't you think? Somebody told him something, or he had a direct involvement at some point."

"That's the most logical explanation. We have a town to explore, let us do that and starting this evening we'll tackle this new video." They finish their breakfast and head out to examine the rest of building three. Five hours in, they discover while sitting at the main security hub that the facility and every building has a name. This facility is Porterhouse. The main street is Daytona Boulevard. Building Three is Coral House, the security hub is Central City, building four is Gable Bay, and the garage is Compton Corners. Alexander mentions his father was from an area known as Compton, California. "Another coincidence," Brooks ponders. Alexander shrugs, but like Brooks, his guard is up. If someone is playing games, he does not find them to be funny.

Upon inspecting the floor plans, the interior design for each building differs, but is similar in that the building seems open until one lives in a section or floor. At that point, the foundation structure changes to allow privacy from outside eyes. Returning their focus to the Central City, Argo shows them all the hidden access points that would lead them to Coral House and Compton Corners and another area, which remained unnamed to them. From the outside there were no visible markers that showed another building, much less its location, yet the floor plans revealed only two avenues and entries to the spot. One entry was reachable from the second floor of the Security Hub, and the second was in a larger suite on the 7th floor at Coral House. They go in search of the two entry points. Upon finding them, they pause and look at each other. At both locations is an enormous sculpture with unusual carvings. Neither sculpture resembles the other in shape, size, or coloring.

Spending several minutes entering every command they had at their disposal, they realize they would need more time to decipher the locks. One decision they made was to share space. They would move into the larger condo with several bedrooms, what appeared to be a media space and the other access entry to their unknown building. Argo returns to Central City to lock the facility, while Alexander and Brooks move the remaining of their belongings from Hondo and the apartment they spent the previous night at. Getting comfortable in front of the media center, they settle into the image of Brooks' father and what new story he was about to share.

The video starts grainy but within seconds becomes sharp and clear. A younger version of her father in appears before the camera. He states his actual name and all the aliases, including Daytona. Daytona explains that here, their current location, is Porterhouse, the facility underground at Quitman Mountains. He gives a brief description of his duties here before he introduces the remaining crew members. As the fourth man introduces himself, Alex jumps from the seat. "That's my father," he exclaims. Both turn to each other puzzled, now wondering if in that their chance meeting was not by accident but fate. They continue listening to her father's time here at the compound, including his responsibilities pertaining to Bayja, an amazing artificial intelligence human, absorbing every detail. After two hours, they break. Both exhausted are full of questions. They agree to turn the conversation to something else, each giving the other an opportunity to review and absorb all that has transpired before asking the tough questions and the history of their families that are now intertwined. They moved from the media center to the patio area. For several minutes neither spoke, they just stared out at the view. Despite its perfection to create a serene environment, neither was calm. Something was bubbling just below the surface, a gigantic storm that they prayed to outrun. They sensed that their very survival was the key to saving hundreds of lives. Breaking the silence Brooks starts, "Wow, despite what my dad is saying, something terrible made him break rank. I wonder if he could get word to your dad because it seems from the conversations, we've had that your dad was on an urgent mission."

Alex nods in agreement. Brooks continues, "each of us has a key to open the Unknown." "Brooks let us wait until we complete the video. Look, my mind is wheeling with all the information we have taken in this evening. We need a couple hours down time to regroup. Feel like a swim?" Agreeing, they both return to their respective rooms to change and make their way to the outdoor pool. Entering the water, they adjust to the coolness and after a few laps felt the heaviness of the day ooze away to the undercurrent of emotions. Each is being to feel about the other. Despite being used to his closeness, Brooks feels an electric charge run through her body when he touches and looks at her. Sensing her uneasiness, he probes, "What's on your mind?"

"Have you ever been in a sexual relationship with a woman?"

"I have."

"Ever been crazy in love or like with one?"

Neither had time nor the inclination to beat around the bush. For all they knew, they were the only humans around. He moves closer within inches, taking her hand and placing it on his heart. "Until I met you, no."

"Sorry to interrupt you two," Argo speaks, springing up from nowhere, "Can you follow me back to Central. We have a problem." Exiting the pool, they all return to Central City. One of the security drones they left in place at Aeverless registered movement inside of the facility. There was an entrance in on the park floor Brooks was not aware of. Their movements were deliberate, as if they knew the layout of the compound and were making their way to the library archives. Brooks gasps a long sigh. Off-hand they counted close to twenty shadows. Knowing he would not like the answer, he asks anyway, "Only a handful of people knew about that entrance, right?"

"Yes, but only one knew how to make their way back in," she confirms. "I wish we knew when the outside perimeter deteriorated. They are looking for something we missed."

"No Brooks," Argo interrupts. "They are looking for you." As if on cue, he types in Bayja on the console and a program starts between two countdowns, a two-hour window and another for twenty-four hours from now. "In two hours, you must deactivate me. You no longer need me and from here on out, I'm a security risk to you."

"What are you talking about," Brooks barks, her voice breaking in anger. The surprises are coming too frequent now. This is not good, as she and Alex need to decide on the fly. No planning or forethought. One wrong move could cost them valuable time or even their lives. "No more games here, Argo. What do you know? All of it spit it out. Tell me the truth now"!

"Your father programmed me to only share information when he felt it was necessary. Certain triggers and keywords selected, so at those critical times, I would provide the help and information you needed. Now you know enough and have enough to move on. You are right, time is of the essence. Tomorrow night you and Alex must leave here. I have two hours to put things in place here. Once you enter the Unknown, you will still have access to certain files and all the information Bayja has compiled. It will lead you to the safe houses and plot your way to Guatemala."

He stops to remove what appears to be two small devices from his skeletal frame. One resembled an archaic thumb drive, and the other was a metal key. "Just prior to the last war," he continues, "your father and his team came together for one last mission to contain a facility in New Region, Utah. Some years prior to that, the government came across some wreckage they first believed was a meteor. To keep from having all the wreckage at one facility, they spread it out throughout Europe and New Region America. The body shipped to Utah, and they sent the hub of the vessel to Aeverless. Senior officials had been conducting an off the books experiment on the body when it went terribly wrong. They killed everyone on site. The team thought they had contained it. When the war broke out, they found out they were wrong. These Shadows are far more advanced than it led them to believe. They adapt and once again they are changing. My physical body is now a danger to you both."

"No," Brooks cries.

"In your heart you know this to be true. You cannot fight me on this, Brooks. This is part of my operating system that is set in stone. You have each other. There is more to the video your father left you. Trust that the information you have will lead you in the right directions and make the choices based on that. Now, I must do what is necessary. Leave me and do what you know you must."

The air in the room seemed as deflated as her mood. "I don't like it, but you're right, Argo. We do not have time to spare. Let us make our way to the Unknown and see what we are working with. We know now that they are intelligent and may have access to other security protocols, we aren't aware of."

She turns to see Alex deep in thought. It was like he was rearranging puzzle pieces in his mind. "Meet me at the Unknown marker on the second floor. I will be there in a few moments." As Alex heads for Coral House, Argo stops him.

"Alex, Brooks," he starts, "I will not be joining you. My journey ends here. Any information you learn from this point forward needs to stay between the two of you.

We can still communicate with each until you enter the Unknown. Once you cross that barrier, my job as your protector is complete." The tears well up in Brooks' eyes. Argo was more than just her protector. He was like her brother, for he had been a part of her life for as long as she could remember. She knew that his job now was to destroy all evidence that she and Alex still existed and to buy them as much time as he could. He hands her the devices and waits for her to deactivate all his history but one, the program which would keep Porterhouse functioning for another two days, and then the program would erase the entire history of any guests from the past fifty years. She leaves the command center, locking Argo and deactivates the elevator system. Walking down to the second floor, she enters and inputs the security codes, locking all doors except for the entrance.

Alex races back to Coral House and grabs his backpack. On his way back, he checks the small pocket. Tucked inside is an unusual metal key, like the one Argo had just revealed. He goes to Brooks' room and grabs her belongings. In her things is a small, unusual charm that she wears around her neck. She had removed it when they went for a swim. He makes his way back to the Unknown marker where Brooks is waiting. The sculpture, which is about three feet wide and three feet tall, resembles a gigantic mass of rock with dozens of symbols and drawings. The surface is both smooth and rough in places, with tiny crevices near the upper right-hand corner. From the monitor Argo tells her where to insert the thumb drive and then turns off all the security cameras except for the garage. She places the thumb drive in the small hole below a symbol resembling a musical half-note as instructed. Her voice cracking, she replies to Argo that it worked and spoke the code words that deactivated the sensor chip that allowed him to correspond with her and Alex.

The rock illuminates a picture on the corresponding wall of the trail leading to the unknown. She sees Alex had collected all their belongings. Neither speak a word. He removes the drive from the rock and takes her by the hand. They head out in silence to the garage. Starting Hondo up, they settle in and push the thumb drive in the half musical note that is now illuminated on the console. The garage goes black and floor lights up like markers to the fifth bay lift. As they approach the bay, the garage door opens. They enter and the bay door shuts behind them. Ahead, another camouflaged door opens, and they drive through. From Central City, Argo is viewing the monitor to the garage. He sees the utility vehicle move and then fade away, leaving the garage empty. He sits in front of the console with another key in his hand. Placing the key in the slot, the counter counts down backwards from 29:00. Twenty-nine hours.

~

For more than an hour, they travel the tunnel with only the headlights on Hondo leading their way. Each still has not spoken a word since leaving Central City, both lost in their own thoughts trying to plan an alternative plan; each digesting the events of the last day and losing their protector and friend Argo. Hondo went into automatic pilot and there was nothing left for them to do but watch. They came across a depot with what appeared to be a train. The doors opened as the utility truck neared. Once the doors opened, Hondo entered and made its way to the halfway point of the train. Still on autopilot, the utility vehicle melded with the train until it was secure, with the front and back opening, allowing easy access to the other cars. As with Hondo, the windows allowed views to the outside, yet from the outside the appearance was pitch black. Any infrared equipment would not detect any living creatures, giving them an advantage once the train left the tunnels. With the train doors closed, the train began moving down the tracks at a comfortable speed. The audio instructs them to the main security center, which is located two cars ahead.

"Welcome, Alex and Brooks. my name is Bayja. The entrance sensors detected your DNA from your fathers, known to me as Compton and Daytona. I worked with your fathers and their teammates to build you a traveling fortress that can withstand any attack, including that of the shadows. I am no longer a physical form but the brain of this vessel. You must have questions? I will do everything in my power to them, about your fathers, the work they did and what we know about the Shadows. My job is to keep you protected. If you would exit at the rear, I will start the tour of your new home and answer questions you may have."

With eyebrows perched, Alex and Brooks make their way to the rear of the car. Brooks was not buying the artificial intelligence story at all. She would keep her comments to herself and share with Alexander later. The doors glided open and shut upon entering the next car. An elevator lift waited. Bayja explains that there are four cars and a maximum of four floors. All the mechanics and hardware that runs Bayja is on the bottom floor. On the second floor is the housing and medical area. The third floor is the greenhouse, leaving the top floor as an observing and logistics area. The train can sustain up to fifty people for five years, reproducing supplies and food as needed.

"Four floors to house fifty people? This isn't a little train at all," Brooks responds. "Why so large?"

"Your fathers wanted to account for if the occupants had families. This vehicle was only to transport essentials the third undisclosed secured location that uninfected could work on a global cure to save humanity," Bayja chimes, her voice cheerful and informative. "There were three missions that your father's and their crew performed together. The first was the initial meeting at Porterhouse. The second was the mission at Dugway, and the third was off the grid. They killed Central four months before the start of the last war in mysterious circumstances. Although the risk was high, the team felt they needed to meet as one of Central's last contacts with me suggested that their mission in Dugway was not complete. Central also discovered that someone had leaked their profiles and there was a mole in the senior official's line of command."

She paused while the two gave great attention to the living quarters, the medical bay. "Should I continue, or do you have specific questions here?"

"Yes," Alex started, "I have one. There does not seem to be a containment or quarantine area. Am I missing something?"

"No," Bayja replies. "There is a fifth car that we can convert if needed. The aim is to not carry anyone or anything that is contaminated. These shadows are much more intelligent than we suspected. With their ability now to morph into your human form and use our knowledge, it is dangerous. This is what your fathers discovered upon Central's death. This vehicle, or vessel, is for the chosen leaders responsible for saving the world. I have picked up the first two passengers. The last transmission that I received from Daytona and Compton was five years ago. Please catch me up on everything that has happened since."

"You said two more passengers?" Alex spoke, beating Brooks to the punch. Bayja intercedes. "Before I can tell you about them, I need to know what has happened to you. Please allow me a little patience; you will understand it all and the criticality of it. My first order is to protect you both, no matter the costs. If the information I learn finds that the other two individuals are not important, or compromised, then we must move on. From your appearance and tone, I can detect that this day has been overwhelming. Rest a while and we will start back up in a few hours. I placed food and garments in your quarters. The quarters, labeled, have symbols on the doors. I have the two of you sharing one apartment. You will recognize yours by something the two of you share in common. Good night, you two. We will resume around 0600." Bayja turns the communication off and monitors their movements to their quarters. She turned off their quarter monitors to allow them downtime without interfering in their privacy. For now, she thought is best that they did not know she was a live human until she heard their story. She runs the monitors from Porterhouse and notices the detonator has clicked down to twenty-two hours.

Their vessel an accumulation of several century old transports: part jet, part train and part submarine. The engineers had thought of every scenario to ensure not only comfort but practicality. There were six floors, two comfortable living areas for up to 100 people. The revised plan was to accommodate the cousins and the families of Central, Compton and Daytona. The off the books' mission came because of Bayja reaching out to them. Her father had a single night affair with her mother and had convinced her to let him raise her solo. He had named her Bayja after their work at Porterhouse. Only Compton and Daytona knew of her existence. After meeting with her father's crew, they brought her to Porterhouse where she had lived. She was fifteen years old. Prior to leaving Porterhouse for the last time, the team spent a month implementing spyware in the remaining facilities that would go undetected, until triggered.

She had no human interaction until Brooks and Alex showed up, but had been another set of eyes that Brooks did not know about. She knew that conversation and her actual appearance would be brutal; one reason she requested they rest. In the end, they would see the reasoning behind it. Bayja hoped they would bond quickly, just as Alex and Brooks had. She sensed that there would always be a deeper bond between the two of them, wondering why they had not tested the water yet. Maybe having them share living space would speed up the process.

Changing to the monitors at Aeverless, she jotted more notes on her tablet and captured images of its new occupants. It took them less than a day to penetrate the external perimeters but two days to figure out how to get inside, even using the entrance that Brooks was not aware. She was proud of the work she and Alex accomplished. They slowed them down. With the booby traps left in place, their numbers will decrease from twenty to less than ten and put a week's maybe two before they get to the external parameters of Porterhouse. By then they would be off in the opposite direction, for reasons that were yet known to her. It is critical that they get there. Their lives and survival of the world depended on it.

~

"How would she know we had something in common? I'm not convinced we are dealing with an advanced AI at all. Most of the remaining ones I have encountered cannot read human interaction unless they are in direct contact with them. Everything in me believes she is human," Brooks spits out, her mind still reeling from the day's events as she and Alex made it to their rooms. Her father working as an undercover operative on covert missions. She wondered if her mother knew anything about that life. They both smile when they come to the door with the dolphin symbol. Placing his hand over the emblem, the door glides open and shuts again behind them. The smell of jerk chicken wafts through the air. In the kitchen is a pot of rice and beans, plantains and steaming chicken. Grabbing a couple of plates and a bottle of wine, they sit down to eat. "Well," Alex smiles, "our fathers did share information with each other about us. Maybe in their offbeat way they are dropping clues to us about each other."

Brooks smiles in agreement. "Still, I think for a computer program to know that much about us. Really," she puffs while stuffing her face. The food was excellent. It reminded her of her mother's cooking, something she did not realize until now that she missed.

"When we first came up on the train platform," Alex goes on in between mouthfuls, "I couldn't see the top of the vehicle. I suspect there maybe another floor or two Brooks, and our Bayja is a perfected AI or very much human, like we are. She is testing our resolve and confirming that we are who we say we are. As you stated when we met, monitors are one thing, but live interaction is something else. So, let us assume she is real. Who is she related to?"

They eat the rest of their meal in silence. Each lost in thought of how the day started and is ending. He reflects to their time at the pool, her question from the night before. "Refill," noticing that her glass is empty. She nods yes, and he fills her glass. "Getting back to our conversation at the pool, you still want my answer," he whispers.

She moves closer to him and lays her head on his shoulder. "I think I know now what your answer is. If we were still at Porterhouse, I would say let us wait because we still have time. For all I know, we could be on board with a shadow who is fattening us up for the kill. If this might be our last night, I want it to mean something. Does that answer your question," she whispers?

They awaken a couple hours later in each other's arms. With their bodies recharged, they put their minds to work with their agenda of questions to ask and places still to see. Until they get the answers they are looking for, they decided they would not leave each other side. They took a shower, ate breakfast and made their way back to the elevator lift. It goes upward instead of back down to the floor where Hondo sits. The space is open. At the center stood a console and a lone woman who rose to greet them. She was small in stature with a mane of the whitest hair they had ever seen.

"Before you start," she starts as she approaches them, "I know maybe I should have introduced myself in person yesterday, but would you have believed me after the heels of losing Argo? You were already struggling with the knowledge of your dad's secret life, and then Alex discovers his father's involvement. Like you, I had a lot of questions back then when I met them. I'm sorry, let me introduce myself, without the urgency in my tone."

They all take a deep breath and sit at the center console. "Good morning," she starts again, her voice pleasant and calm. "My name is Bayja Morrows. I am the daughter of Central City. Upon my father's death, your fathers moved me to Porterhouse. They considered it to be the safest place I could be."

"Okay, Bayja," Brooks interrupts for the moment. There was something familiar about her. They shared the same eyes. Another sign to Brooks that there were more secrets about her life. Dismissing the thought, she inhales and begins her dissection "Nice to meet you. Let us cut the chitchat and get to work. Since time is of the essence, let us share some facts. You need to confirm in person who we are. Fine, run your protocol."

Bayja gazes at the fire bug in front of her. Brooks does not mince words or waste time. "I like you are direct and to the point. Okay, I get it. What I need is for all of us to review each other's background again. For me to hear first-hand and for us to connect some dots. For all the cloak and dagger, our fathers had a reason this was important to them."

"Fine," Brooks responds. "I'll go first." For the next hour Brooks went over every detail of significance, starting with her introduction to Alex back almost three years before she took a break. Listening, Bayja took no notes, she only listened. She rose briefly to cross the room, retrieving beverages and fresh fruit. She returned to the console and Brooks began again, detailing from the death of her parents back to her first memories of Aeverless. Scanning the room, she spies a large timepiece reading ten hours, fifteen minutes and thirty-nine seconds.

Inhaling, she asks for the restroom. Bayja points to the corner of the room. Alex rises with her and stands outside the door until she finishes. They return to the console together. "And your story," Bayja asks as Alex sits back down.

Alex begins from his time growing up in Chicagoland. Until he was ten, despite the hardship and challenges of the war and virus outbreak, his family could remain there with some since of order. His father had risen from the rank of beat cop to running vice division, while his mother was a prominent physician. He talks about his father's regiment training that he required everyone in his household to take part in every single day. At first, he thought it had to do with his dad's job as a police officer, but in hindsight he was training them for battle, a veritable war he knew was coming. He talks about why they left there and headed west towards Oregon.

"Why Oregon," Bayja inquires, her silver mane swaying as she tilts her head. Alex continues to state that they were rumors his father heard that there was a town of uninfected people living there free from roaming dead or shadows. Bayja records this information on her tablet. "From what I knew of your fathers, nothing they did was casual. Every decision made, planned and calculated. There had to be a reason. Did you ever make it there?" she responds.

"No, we didn't. There was an ambush from some infected animals in New Nebraska. The infection spread, killing my parents and siblings. I continued with another family and we made it as far as Montana. There was talk about Guatemala having vessels off the coast that were free from infection. I was one of a few people chosen to investigate. The others went to check out sites off the coast of New World, California, and Canada.”

“Do you remember the route you followed before you ended up in Aeverless,” Bayja counters. “Somewhere along that route you may have triggered one of their alarms. It would be great if we can figure that out. We can mimic it, or at least see where they have sentries on guard. What do you remember about Oregon? Did he give you a name or description? I’m sorry,” she pauses as she looks at their facial expressions. “Let me explain by telling you my story. Like your father’s had daily training sessions, so did mine. Unlike the two of you, my father was the only family I knew. We moved around, spending a couple of months in some city, then several months in rural areas that had little habitation. Looking back now, it was my dad’s way of conditioning me to be alone. I was fifteen when my dad died, four months before the war started.”

“Wait,” Alex chimes in. “You’ve been at Porterhouse since you were fifteen? Don’t you find it weird that your father named you after the AI?”

“He didn’t. To be honest, I cannot say what his motives were. Maybe he thought the information or transition for us to go from skeptical to trusting would be easier. And yes, I’ve been here alone since fifteen.” Bayja takes a deep breath and sighs before continuing. “In his belongings, he left me a few weird items: a phone number, a handful of skeleton keys, and a phrase.

Calling the phone number connected me with your fathers and the cousins. They made their way to me and brought me to this place. It is strange because when I arrived it was like my father had painted a picture of this place. Every inch I knew intimately. They spent a couple of weeks here getting me acclimated."

She stops to catch her breath while drinking some water. It had been a long time since she had a full conversation with other humans, and in her eagerness to bring them up to speed, she was becoming hoarse. They give her a few minutes before Alex asks, "This phrase you mentioned. What was it?"

She starts, "I know my heavens aren't pearly. We gave them with streets of pain. To reach my heavens, I must seal the gates in vain."

"For tomorrow I will shout from my haven, oh Lord forgive our souls. Take my Garden of Eden to glory, and leave my earth unscorched and known," Alex adds.

"For if daisies could be orchids and the sea became my haven, I would never have another care in the world. Only love and my salvation will be among my loyal companions to help lead me to the end," Brooks completes. "The overhead monitor splits between the counting counter and a grainy video featuring Compton, Daytona, and the cousins. At first glance, there were no visible indications or signs to their location, only the date stamp March 18, 2259."

The taller of the two cousins looks into the camera and speaks. "Alex, Bayja and Brooks, we hope that you all are now together. If you are not, then you are in the locations of where we left this video. At the time of this recording, you are the three oldest of our banded family. My cousin and I do not have children, nor have never married and are the only surviving members of our family. I know we are asking more of you than we should, but please believe me, we will make sure you are as prepared as possible for the fight ahead. You will need to rely on each other only as the leadership going forward, no matter who else may join you, for you are the only ones with all the markers we have left to guide you to safety. This team is not random. Nothing about our meeting or working together was coincidental. Each of you holds separate pieces of the puzzle. Some parts are phrases, some keys, and our recordings. We talked a lot about Guatemala, but Central discovered something that each of us was not aware of. We have a similar DNA marking, making us immune to certain diseases but a threat to the original DNA markers of the shadows. There is a facility in Oregon, a depot with weapons we have left for you. Make that your first stop. We will talk more when you get there. We love you. God speed."

At the end of the video, the console pipes "Information loaded. Voice markers confirmed and activated." Bayja explains it records their voices and nuances, allowing them to run console from anywhere on the vessel. They gear the vessel to be self-sufficient. She explains from the observation floor they can view their surroundings and rarely should one of them have to be at controls. They can spend most of their time in observation. They design the seating for comfort. There was also a gym and a full kitchen for their convenience. The structure and metal framing were years of combination between the alien ship found and innovative technology. This vessel will allow them to travel undetected during evening hours. During daylight, they would need to mimic the environment in order to remain undetected.

"There's something I need to explain before we proceed," Bayja cautioned. "No need," they chime simultaneously. "We figured there were other alarms activated by who initialized them. We suspect that someone who left Aeverless in search of a new facility ran into the Shadows and the information ended up being compromised."

"You are close in your speculation. Leaving Porterhouse early than we needed will put at least two weeks' lead time between us and the Shadows. Between your traps and mine, it will take them time to figure out which direction you went. If we can cut this crew in half, that would be even better. I have a film on that as well. We will know when they will either back track out of Aeverless or find your trail. The detonations in some tunnels will take them time to get through." She stops for another glass of water.

"Bayja," Alex interjects, "one thing to buy us some time as well was we laid a false trail to Abilene."

She smiles. "That's perfect. Let us pray it works. One other thing," she begins again. "After their last completed mission, our fathers discovered that one of the off-grid agencies breached several security measurements and uncovered their actual identities and some missions it involved them in. Thankfully, none could not discover their locations, apart from my father. Your fathers and the cousins laid deep cover in their whereabouts. Brooks, no one knew your father's proper name, but they identified the other four men he toured with. That is to our advantage, as your identity to this group is unknown. There is a video I will bring up later and we can review it together. Besides the shadows, this director may be our deadliest enemy. Take some more downtime, you both deserve it. I will need you up to speed and at full capacity once we go above ground. Our fight starts then, continuous offensive. Playing catch up will cost us our lives."

~

Back at Central City, as the acid peels away at the inner workings of flesh and circuitry, Argo moves to finish the last command from Daytona, given many years ago. Returning to the medical lab, he removes three small vials of blood, breaks them in various locations, leaving small amounts of blood trails. Fifty feet from the train depot, he takes his last step. His body disintegrates, leaving no traces to rebuild.

The Shadows

Outside of Dugway Proving Grounds, New Region
Utah - Year 2211

A lone rancher was settling his horses for the night when a fiery flame hurled from the sky outside of Salt Lake City. Remnants of it landed over a two-hundred-mile radius. The man lived just outside of Dugway and the old Army Proving Ground, which had sat vacant now for over seventy years. He watched with great interest as a piece of what he thought to be a meteor landed on his ranch. He was proud of the hundred and sixty acres passed down several generations to him. Gathering his weapon, he made his way to his vehicle and drove to the point of contact. The closer he got, the worse the stench became. About a mile from the crash site, he stopped. The smoke was so heavy, he could barely see, much less breathe. He called the local sheriff and reported what he saw, backed up another mile from the crash and waited. Fifty feet from his position a shadow shifted in the woods watching the man in the truck. The crash had startled him as he was illegally on the rancher's property. With the smoke increasing filling his eyes and lungs he turned south, heading towards one of the six man-made lakes on the property. He paused for a second as he felt something sting his neck. Swiping at it, he continued his way. Best to lie low for a while, so he retreated to his hiding spot and watched the excitement unfold.

Ninety minutes passed before the local law enforcement and what appeared to be some soldiers from the closest military facility pulled up in large tank like vehicles. A chopper flew in from the south and landed about 100 to 300 feet from them. A couple of men got out of the chopper, wearing these weird silver suits, and approached his vehicle. He pointed toward where he thought the rock landed. They turned to the tanks and headed toward the heavy smoke. The sheriff and another gentleman in a fancy suit accompanied him back to his ranch. They cautioned it was for his security, but he knew better. They did not want any word leaking out about the crash. Only seemed appropriate, as he had a son serving in the Arm Corp. Several weeks passed before the team of man cleared his property. Each evening he could see the tanks coming and going from the area they had lit up like a Christmas tree with full decorations. Around the third week, for eight straight days, several choppers lifted pieces of ground and whatever it was. He knew then that it was more than just some meteor, but he knew not to ask. He just kept his mouth shut and minded his business as if they were not there. At the end of the fifth week, they informed him that the crash site and the surrounding ten miles radius was now property of the government. They handed him a fat check and a non-disclosure form to sign. He accepted, halfway grateful and relieved that they were leaving his property and not seizing all of it. Another few weeks went by and he continued to see vehicles come and go. They were shielding the site from the entrance in every direction. Week nine was when things got a little hairy. Slowly the animals started getting ill, lethargic and dying. He did not call the local vet, but the lone number left by the gentleman in the fancy suit. He showed back at his doorstep within two hours. The rancher thought nothing of it, but he should have. That would have told him that the government did not go far and had his ranch under surveillance since the crash. Fancy suit inquired of the rancher if something connected his current irrigation system to each of the lakes. He nodded yes in compliance. Again, a couple of tanks showed with the men in the silver suits. They took water and soil samples surrounding his barn and home. At the end of their study, they marked the entire ranch as property of the government, with giant no trespassing signs. The rancher had died. In his hiding place, the trespasser was barely alive. The changes in his appearance were hideous and his DNA was transforming. He lived another three weeks before the men in the hazmat suits and fancy suit came and took him away. The chopper flew a short distance before landing again in an underground facility. Fancy suit made his way from the landing spot to the bank of elevators. His phone chimes as he stops short of the elevator. He gives the standard response before confirming that the rancher and the trespasser resembled a similar case reported in New Kentucky in 2195.

~

December 2256–sixty miles west of Noah's Ark, New Utah

From their designated meeting spot, Central waited in silence for the rest of the crew to arrive. He had been fishing off a pier in San Diego when he received word of this new assignment. From the frequent communication he received from the AI at Porterhouse, he learned that he and the cousins were still single. Compton and Daytona had wives and were starting families. For five years past their time at Porterhouse, each had solo missions they did not discuss, but he suspected as the rest it correlated them. He found it odd that almost twenty years later it summoned them to come together for this mission. Right on schedule, each arrived with Daytona, the last leading the pack. They all sized each other up, with the years piled on none had lost or added to their physical appearance except Central. He had slimmed down about forty pounds, which only made his once stocky frame more compact. He now had the body of a well-chiseled tank. After a quick catch up, each member relayed their piece of the assignment. They were to contain a situation, by any means necessary, at the old Dugway Proving Ground, now known in the senior agencies as Noah Ark's.

Since the late 2100's, more experimentation involving ancient and current DNA structures experiments were being conducted. Some to prevent disease and then the most obvious to conspiracy theorists to develop and prevent bioterrorism. Forty years ago, a meteor crashed in the New North America and Old Europe. Soldiers discovered a tremendous piece outside of Salt Lake City, and in the wreckage, they discovered an alien skeleton. They distributed pieces of the cartilage among several covert facilities, with the alien form staying close to ground zero. Dugway had been vacant for over seventy years, but with the new discovery, they enhanced it to secure the most secretive projects the government was working on. The only other facility with this much security and secrecy was Aeverless, which was in the former state of New Mexico. While they rumored it that Aeverless worked on the technology found at the crash site, Noah's Ark continued to conduct several experiments of the DNA with soil, animal and human samples, both healthy and compromised. A critical error, made by one of the junior biologists, ended up infecting about forty percent of the staff.

After planning the attack, the group inspects their equipment, including hazmat gear, before setting off for Noah's Ark. From start to finish, the mission took fourteen hours. They submitted their report to the officials; however, each knew beyond any doubt that it had played them. By design, the senior officials had set them up for failure as, no one mentioned the missing culprit and his team of scientists. Somehow, they knew about the upcoming raid. There was a leak somewhere, and they intended on plugging it. They survived this mission. Going underground was the only way they would stay alive. The crew spent the next several weeks days holed up discussing every solo mission they performed since their stay at Porterhouse. They planned they would activate when the time came necessary. Each would continue to use the Bayja protocol, which was only known by the five of them. None would be privy to the others location, as they had elected to follow since leaving Porterhouse. Daytona moved to the inner city of the New York Burroughs, while Compton left California and made his way to Chicagoland. The cousins went off grid to Old Canada. Central made his made south towards Guatemala. By March 2257, the crew began laying the groundwork for the survival of the world as they knew it.

~

Noah's Ark March 2257

From the depths of his impenetrable lab, fancy suit and his team of scientists continued their experiments on the latest skeletal form of the DNA. They had guarded the alien for the past sixty years. The senior officials thought they had eradicated the problem, but failed to keep the funding for his team in check. Through a myriad of smoke and mirrors, he built another containment lab on the old ranch grounds once it was livable again. Two months before the covert attack, someone notified him of the impeding attack. He moved the entire team and installed cameras at the

Noah's Ark to watch the day-to-day on-goings.
Whoever the demolition team was that they sent in,
they were good. Using his extensive resources, he could
identify all five members, yet very little information on
each of them since 2237. That team of five reminded
him of ghosts, hiding in plain sight yet deadly. He
would keep digging for any information he could find.
Information was power, and he knew they were a direct
threat to him and his goals.

In 2211, he was a young covert agent on his sixth
assignment. Little did he know that mission would
propel his career to be one of the most revered and
feared covert agency director. From the beginning, he
was ambitious and radical in his approach. Initially,
senior officials loved that about him, but as his
direction at Noah's Ark became more ominous, they
had to contain him. Fancy suit was an arduous studier
of history and believed that fate, not luck, awarded him
that night back in 2211. The advances that his team
took and made in bioterrorism made him not only a
threat to his own country, but marketable to any country
wanting his service. But he was a patriotic man, his
allegiance was to make and keeping his country as a
superpower. He wanted everyone to fear them and bow
down to any demands that they made.

Through years of testing, they discovered that the alien
skeletal was volatile and adapting. When he had first
seen the life-form some forty years ago, the first thing
that stuck out in his mind was how translucent the skin

was, even though they could not penetrate it with their weapons. It had spiny vertebrae and razor-like claws that appeared to be the hands and feet. The body did not appear to have any teeth but somehow could transfer part of the DNA makeup with anything it stung. It reminded him of a shadow in the darkness; it is creepiest at the darkest hour before dawn. In the beginning, he could not understand how the trespasser became infected. Several years passed before they cracked how the rancher became infected and died. He also found interesting that when the infected host could not handle the invasion, it would collect the marrow and lay dormant until mated with another host.

Five years ago, they made a breakthrough from a snafu in the lab. Adhering to the security protocols was fancy suit's number one rule. Errors in the lab causes chaos, and chaos among the shadows resulted in death. They required everyone to wear hazmat gear from the feet to the scalp, including hands was crucial to prevent infection. Before and after each shift, they inspected all gear for tears. One of the lab technicians got lazy and did not inspect their gear. They had a tear in their gloves and while transporting a small dormant sample; they became infected. Until that time, most infected humans had died within a two-month period. The quarantined tech however was still alive, even though the DNA had morphed his skeletal bones in just six months. At the time they assumed it was something in their DNA that the shadow required but had not found. This was the breakthrough that fancy suits were looking for. He could now breed a super warrior incapable of injury. Fancy suits did not realize just what he had done. This was a colossal error on his part; a deadly one that would start the war and infection and change the course of their survival forever.

The Present–Aeverless

Jonas Strangelove followed the shadows into the compound known as Aeverless. It had taken his father, fancy suit, several years to discover its existence, but he could not get the exact coordinates to locate it. A stroke of genius in planting the triggers and following the lone traveler from a distance more than a month ago, along with retrieval of an Aeverless occupant, incubated in Abilene, gave him the coordinates he needed. Someone had rescued the traveler before his minions could infect him, thus setting them back several weeks before venturing here again. With that, he lost the mark. Upon entering the facility, it disappointed him as the mark and his rescuer appeared to have long gone.

Although fancy suit was not Jonas' biological father, he considered the man to be the only father he knew. Growing up in a broken home filled with violence and drugs, he made his escape to serve his country at 15. His instincts with weaponry and combat fighting moved him up the ranks, and with recommendations from his superiors he transferred from non-commissioned to commission. He was a firm believer that every circumstance happens for a reason. Jonas volunteered to become part of the fancy suit's security detail and even took part in the cloning experiment. He was the first successful cross bred of the two species, human and alien. Even with the strange side effects, Jonas knew it meant him great things, power beyond his wildest imagination. No longer considering himself human, he was the alpha Shadow and every clone after him was under his command.

He wished his father were still alive to see the place. A great deal of care went into destroying as much of it as possible. It satisfied him that his technology would pull out the information he needed. Off the grid, this would make a perfect facility for cloning, so his next step would be to rebuild and change to his specifications. When the information trickled back about spotting a girl, his first guess was they had found Morrows daughter, but from the images captured revealed that was not the case. She was younger, like the man, both unknown to him. There attempts to locate any other members of the crew had also been empty. Unlike his father, he suspected that somehow communications got out to them, and with it they could retrieve Morrows' daughter, and all went underground. Another scenario would be that either during the war or at the onset of the viral attack, they met their demise. Now it did not matter. His concerns were on this place and the girl that had inhibited it. He assumed she had lived here or how else would she have found and known about the place. Even the previous occupant, some girl name Ava, knew nothing of the girl on the screen. Three straight days they scoured every inch of the facility, finding no traces of DNA anywhere. Every security program code Ava had was no longer viable. Either the girl had been here a while and worked around the security and installed new programs, or there were some fail-safe measures in place to secure the site and information stored here upon evacuation. Humans would have done the later. He learned they worked best in a defensive mode instead of offensive. Day five, he found his first thread through a small lens planted within a water deprived fern. They had adjusted the temperature of the facility to allow the Shadows' free movement about the premise. When the ferns shattered from the extreme cold, they found one had a secure lens. The recording looked to be only a couple of weeks old, showing the lone traveler and girl moving back and forth between the area and another door they were yet to discover until now. Using the humans' technology paired with the Shadows, he ran diagnostics until a facial recognition and DNA matched the traveler to the crew member known as Hennessey Whitehouse, but no match of the girl. They followed their movements to the large freezer like door on the third floor. He gave orders for them to move out and find the two humans. He would remain here with a couple of Shadows to complete the rebuild, including a new cloning device. With what he had seen of the terrain, it would be a couple of days before the team would be back with his prey.

~

Present Day–Aboard Hondo.1

From the console, the three of them watched in silence as the Shadows discovered the lens in the living quarters at Aeverless. They paid attention to the Shadow with distorted human features, minus the hands which always looked to remain covered. Bayja had brought them up to speed, filling in as many gaps as she could. Everything new sighting of the Shadows had been up linked to their database. With the new images, they can study them. To prevent intrusion of the recording capability still maintained at Aeverless, the cousins could provide more detail in the video feeds. They even added new schematics to changing disguise of their vehicle, which was lovingly called Hondo dot one. Hondo dot one designed to get them to Oregon. From there, another transport with more advanced weaponry would chart their next course of action and destination.

As Bayja had predicated, they now have a good three-week advantage. Deciphering the clues, they determined that their next destination was over sixteen hundred miles from Porterhouse. The tunnels routed them underground, crossing into the World of Mexico back in America's New Mexico. From there they had several hundred miles of desert driving, which was perfect for Hondo One. All Intel filtered into their database showed that the desert was the least place they would run into the Shadows. There were limited places to hide from the scorching sun during light hours. Upon arriving in New Mexico, day two since leaving Porterhouse, in the early morning hours, they found that the war had a heavy effect on the climate. Instead of scorching heat, it was blistering cold, almost artic. With the roaring winds, the wind chill set the temperature reading to almost thirty-five below Fahrenheit. It also did not help that the sky lit up every few hours in a painful dance of electricity and pummeling hail. It took most of one day to make the adjustments to the motors and shielding, most of which being accomplished in the open. As the shadows preferred cold temperatures, making a return trip back through New Mexico was no longer an option. All three assumed that their journey, to Guatemala, would contain detours to distract any followers from learning their true destination. After making their rounds and setting the navigation to drive through the night, they settled at the console to make the obvious corrections that they had already encountered and review the latest counterintelligence from the hidden devices left at Aeverless.

Despite their best efforts to slow them down, they discovered the Shadows had plans for Aeverless. Rebuilding was taking place. The Shadows intended to use the facility for what they did not quite know. Knowing that other Shadows had died there, the three of them surmised it was just a matter of time before the Shadows discovered the same. If the Shadows could revive the dead tissues, it would increase their community and bring them closer to identifying Brooks' ancestry. It was imperative that they make it to

Oregon quickly, with no further delays. They watched as the lead Shadow scurried from section to section, examining every piece of floor and wall for clues for any human existence. With the terrain differing from the maps, they spent more time navigating through the ridges and crevices of the land. It would be difficult for humans to make permanent shelter here, but the Shadows could make this environment work to their advantage.

Day three of their voyage started off ordinary. Brooks was on deck monitoring the roadways when an internal alarm pinged at the console station. From their stations they watched as the Shadows broke into the catacomb where the infected had laid. As if on cue, the transmission went black and a grim video of Daytona appeared and began signing.

"If you are seeing this, the seal to the catacomb has broken. Despite our best efforts to contain the infection, they have been able to go dormant. This is the last transmission that you will receive from this facility. Change all your security coordinates and protocols now, quickly. The Shadows have infused themselves into technology and have telepathic signatures. At the time of this recording, I remain uninfected, but I fear that will now change as they will want vital information about all progress, we have made in learning their technology. I'll try to hold them off as long as possible to buy you more time." The screen goes blank. A few minutes pass before Alex and Bayja join her on the observation deck. Bayja signs "wow," while Alex signs "Amazing."

"So, our fathers," Bayja starts, "it seems developed a way of communicating between them that was undetectable to anyone else."

"It looks that way," Alex agrees. "At least we are familiar with it and can rely on it. It explains why Argo could not complete this journey with us. So now we are blind to any additional on-goings at Aeverless. We assume it will only be a matter of time or days before they pick up our trail. I'm hoping that our fathers made some precautions too that will at least alert us if they find Porterhouse."

Bayja assures them they did, and they would get a notification once it happens. She knew they would find the facility. Her concern, like the others, was that they would be secure at their new facility in Oregon working on the next piece of the puzzle. Still, they needed to plan for unforeseen contingencies like the one they encountered with the terrain in New Mexico. Checking the coordinates, they had another five hundred miles to go before reaching their destination. Taking the advice of Brooks' father, they run the execution program and change all the security applications to their vital equipment and databases. They both turn to Brooks, who had been quiet since they joined her. Sensing their concern, she offers her thoughts.

"The message he left. Alex, you have the photographic memory. Did you see anything out of the ordinary? Bayja, you knew him and out of all of us has the most insight. Do you see anything, or am I just stretching for something that isn't there?" she sighs.

Alex mentions that at the end of the video before it fades, Daytona seemed to relay a series of numbers. "7 2 4 9 7 1," Bayja confirms. "I noticed," she continues, "that neither of you came on board with a locker. When I was traveling with your fathers, and when they left Porterhouse, each of them had a small portable locker." Turning to leave the deck, she motions for them to follow her back to her quarters. From the bedroom, she retrieves a small locker. "My dad carried this everywhere we went." She opens the locker to show them some encrypted maps and a couple of unusual keys. "I knew the combination in my sleep. I suspect that if your fathers did not have them in their possession that somewhere on our journey, something will trigger a memory of where they might be. Do either of you recognize the numbers," she asks?

Brooks responds she does not, however Alex is familiar with the six digits. "When I was little, my father would take me to the aquarium. He used to make me memorize the markings of every seventh tank. There were 249 steps from the street to our front door. And the precinct my father worked at was on 71st street. It is a key to something. If your father knew it," turning his attention to Brooks, "then my father or maybe of the other fathers must have your key Brooks."

Present day Aeverless

Finding the entrance to the catacomb, the Shadows retrieved the dormant cells of their patriots. Jonas makes his way to the single containment that was separate from the cells of the others. After a gestation period of a few days, he could replace the members he was losing in the tunnels leading out of the facility. Only two remained, and they were building a gateway to cross the deep ravine they encountered at the end of one tunnel.

At the end of the catacomb was a containment area, clawed heavily by his patriots. They could not penetrate it while they were alive. Something, however, broke the barrier and it opened the door. He concluded it opened when the humans vacated sometime within the last month. In the corner sitting in a chair was the remains of a skeletal male. Upon further inspection, it disappointed him that the bones had become crystallized. Their ability to abstract any DNA would be minimal, not allowing them the ability to fuse their structure or much less determine who the dead man was. Despite the setback, the remains left him a valuable prize. They recovered a small video recorder of the man known as Daytona, from the crew responsible for destroying Dugway. This was good news. Even better was the small two-way monitoring they detected. Summing his comrades, they went to work on detecting where the video feed is transmitting to.

Present Day–Winema National Park, Oregon

Hondo One perched on the tip of the forest's entrance in complete stealth mode undetected. Its passengers apprehensive about moving forward well after darkness, but sitting in the open was not a good option either. From the New Mexico to Oregon, the texture of the land is constantly changing. The only constant was the frigid temperatures. They opted to enter from the southeast border of Nevada, where they had more desert cover than forest. At the start of the 21st century, Winema and Fremont National Forest became one gigantic national forest with over two million acres of land. The coordinates left by their fathers were specific, right down to the landmarks. The fear of missing a landmark, coupled with the possibility of running into Shadows and/or mutated animals, either of which they did not want to lead to their new hideaway. They sent out sensor probes and wait.

They had just shut down all the engines but two, when Hondo readjusted the lights and camouflage and advised its passengers to return to their protective gear, retrieve the sealed backups labeled with their names on them from sick bay, and return to the utility vehicle. Radar had detected another fierce storm approaching within the hour. The storm would help lay cover as they traveled inward towards their destination. Knowing time was of the essence, they obeyed, and each was secure in their seats in the original vehicle within 15 minutes.

The utility vehicle then detached itself from the main train and backed itself out through the opening doors that had remained shut since leaving Porterhouse. The train then powers itself down and starts security measures, disinfecting and disintegrating everything to remove all traces of DNA, all the while securing itself from probes or attacks. Hondo moves forward and begins moving into the dense sea of molded trees and rocks covered in heavy ice. Reading the landscape, the database adjusted the armor, and followed the sound of the sensors sent ahead. No one spoke a word, and the vehicle moved at a steady pace. As the storm continued to move closer, the temperature kept falling from–15 to–60 before stabilizing. A few hours passed before the vehicle stops at the base of a vast mountain. The sensors aligned themselves back to the side of the armor. The navigator asked Alex for the six-digit password they learned from Daytona's last video. After reciting the last digit a few minutes pass before the vehicle starts up again and moves forward in what appears to be a dim cave. Successfully crossing the barriers, total darkness surrounds them. Hondo travels another two to three miles before another set of steel doors appear before them. The navigator then asks Bayja to place the yellow key in her possession inside the mechanical arm. She does so, and the arm detaches from Hondo and barrels up the left side of the door and places the key in the allotted slot and turns. It takes several minutes for the doors to open. The arm retrieves the key and returns to its base. The vehicle creeps into the shaft, waits for the doors to close, and after several more minutes it begins its descent into the mountain.

Unbeknownst to them, another storm was brewing behind them at the site where they left the train. A deep slime of black mold crawled its way up, encompassing the train. Sharp pedipalps tapped at the armor until it snaked its way inside the hull, sliding down the walls at an expedient rate. Reaching the floor, the mold took on a strange shape and then disseminated through the train in search of prey. Seeing that no one was aboard, it moaned in anger, having missed the humans. It found the darkest space and waited.

Unlike their smooth entry at Porterhouse, this ride was painful and slow. The sides resembled an old pulley system, and the gears creaked from the weight of the vehicle. On the floor were to be dollies and hand carts used in the 20th century. There were small readings of radon, even though uranium had stopped being farmed since the mid-21st century. From their first glance, the elevator appeared to be part of a mine shift. The elevator lightening wasn't the greatest, the only illumination coming from the vehicle's exterior lights against a heavy door of steel combined with some weird rubber like substance like tar, but it seemed to be slicker in texture as nothing could adhere itself to the surface.

They continued down the mountain, gears continuing to creak for over sixty minutes. A sudden shutter of hitting the ground informed them that this part of the ride had ended. The heavy doors open, and the sensors once again detach themselves from the position the glides forward providing adequate light. Ahead of them is another bridge gateway, only this like the shaft is remnant of the past. Concrete pillars and simple wood and tile panels graced the floor. All three look quizzically at each other, uncertain that the weight of Hondo would cross gracefully. They were wrong; the vehicle ramped up and crossed as if it had entered a speedway and was being challenged for the best time. After crossing the electronic arms detached and set chargers to detonate within 20 minutes. In front of them, another barrier door had opened. With the sensors and arms back in place, Hondo moves again towards the first set up glass doors. As the vehicle approaches, the door open and close when the vehicle is in place. From the ceiling, a mist descends as the navigator inside Hondo explains the vehicle is undergoing the final containment screening.

Bayja speaks first. "Well, it looks like our way in will definitely not be our way out. And what's with the ancient throwback mechanics and technology?"

"Others, especially the Shadows, cannot hack the transportation so easily," Alex begins. "Therefore, our fathers found that using the throwbacks during their travel to their vantage. From the looks of it, we will need to use it as well." The system interrupts and asks them each to remove their protective gear and place it in the incinerator and then exit the vehicle to the second quarantine room ahead on their left.

They followed the instructions and proceeded to the room as requested. They spent the next thirty minutes bathing a few times to include the washing of their hair. After each washing, there was a chiming of a bell and after the fourth chime, the doors to the quarantine opened to another hall. They placed great care in attempting to make the space breathable, despite being several hundred yards underground. Their guess that it at one point was an old mining facility proved accurate, and old signs appeared on the walls referencing caution and protective gear. They had painted the walls outside of the glass at some point. Streaks of white and yellow still stained, but the place to Brooks felt claustrophobic. She hopes their time here is brief. They came into another opening circular. Heavy glass doors sealed them in. There were four rooms apart from the hall they just exited. A control room, the open space which had a kitchen facility, two bedrooms and a greenhouse. Each of the bedrooms had an open living area, a bathing area, and four decent size beds. In the storage space was clothing appropriate to their new environment. To the right of the greenhouse was another door leading to an area not yet cleared for them.

They congregated in the control room and entered the credentials requested at the console. For Bayja, it was the name of the city her father and she visited on her 10th birthday. For Brooks, it was the author of her mother's favorite book, and it required Alex to enter his favorite color. The console hums for a few minutes before the entire place lights up. "Welcome to Argo, Brooks, Bayja, and Alex. We will limit your stay here, only a few weeks, but there is a lot to learn. In the back of each bedroom and the greenroom is an exit. There is a mining cart that will transport you back and forth through the tunnels. Each exit end routes to the same tunnel. Be sure to gather as many supplies as you can. To get them to your next mode of transportation, each of you will need to travel separate, hence the mining carts. I would suggest resting for a couple of days and read up on the material we will be reviewing. Then load up and take a few days getting the supplies onboard Hondo Three. On your last day, I will instruct you how to remove my structure from the console and how to upload it once aboard the Hondo. Last, there is a cabinet labeled medication. Be sure each of you take two tablets daily. Your body will need to readjust from being so far underground and adjust to the new altitudes. Eat, get a good night's sleep and we'll start early in the morning."

The three of them took another look around the room at their new quarters. Despite being underground, Aeverless and Porterhouse afforded them comforts this spot did not. From first inspection, there was not an outdoor area infused with natural light. There were not several floors allowing for space. Maybe that was the point being conveyed. This is a mission for survival, not a picnic. For Brooks, everything about this place did not set well with her. Despite every security precaution, she felt they were being watched. They made their way to the kitchen area and found food like rationing that the military and aerospace gave to their crew. Alex, to lighten the situation, cracks at least the food did not look and taste like vomit. The affect works as they relax and begin talking about the storm and the venture into the mountain.

"I wonder," Brooks begins, "how they kept this place a secret. It looks as if they meant to use it for mining, but then changed the structure for an underground emergency bunker. I do not know about you all, but this place makes me feel way out of sorts, almost blinded. I have no inkling how far underground we are, and from the looks of it, our security measures are quite limited."

"Um," Alex starts and then pauses, "I somewhat agree, but I think once we see what is on the other side of the doors, we may have better security measures than we think. The console is telling us our time here is short. Maybe there is an internal clock that starts ticking tomorrow morning that we must adhere to. The fathers' said that this was a pit stop only to get supplies and nothing more. I suspect the more is for our unfriendly guests who want nothing more than to wipe us off the face of the earth. What do you think, Bayja?"

Nodding, she begins, "I don't like this place either. I wish we could get started tonight, but let us get the rest we need. I am curious, however, why all of our belongings were to remain onboard Hondo One." Brooks, feeling somewhat claustrophobic, had been walking around the space, taking slow concise breaths, trying not to hyperventilate. She pauses in front of the greenhouse and stares for several minutes before turning and smiling to the group. "Hey guys, come here and look," she motions them forward. They join her at the entrance and stare into the room. After several moments, both shrug in confusion. "Look at the wall art," she points upward, "at the 40 degree and 90-degree mark in this room. Do you see it now?"

The patterns were like the lobby statues at Porterhouse. Standing at the exact replicas opened a hidden panel in the greenhouse. Journals and logs from their fathers about the mission at Dugway. "Great find Brooks," Bayja smiles. "Let's see if there are any others." They search the primary room, along with the two bedrooms bringing their total of fourteen journals dated between the Dugway mission and the months prior to the war, their rescue of Bayja and their last visit here. Here, they referred as Winema. Feeling the effects of the day, they all turned in and awoken a few hours later, renewed. As instructed, each opens the doorway to the tunnels from their respective bedrooms and greenhouse to find a steel mine cart at their disposal. The cart resembled a small box truck with enough store space to fill a two-bedroom-living quarter, including a living area and kitchen. In each exit were boxes and crates, wrapped airtight and labelled in her father's sign language. Giving a code to her partners, they could decipher what each box encompassed, ammo, medicines, food supplies, bedding and clothing. The ammo and food crates were many, leading them to wonder why they needed so many supplies.

After loading their carts, each made their way down the tunnel. The mile tracker read twenty-five miles before approaching the entrance of another vehicle, similar but different from Hondo One. Tirelessly, they loaded their inventory and equipment onboard, noting that the vehicle's primary use was for storage. The console area with the controls to the vehicle had comfortable seating with a galley area dedicated for kitchen and bathroom use. They kept this pace up for five days, with each evening dedicated to reading the journals. At the end of the fifth evening, the monitor confirms their job is complete. It instructed them to put on their protective gear, exit from the greenhouse doors and to make their way to Hondo B. As the mine cart left the bay, they hear a countdown begin. *Time to detonation 4:59:58.* Onboard the vehicle, still wearing their protective gear, they secure themselves in their seats as the vehicle takes off careening down the ramp way at a high rate of speed. With the coordinates already pre-set, they set off again, this time for the unknown.

~

With the facility now operational for mass cloning, Jonas was unhappy. The lead to the two missing humans had gone cold. The recording device had also been a waste of time. It was archaic, and they had found no information on its existence. The cost of following the tunnels in search of them had cost him both labor and colleagues. Based on the information he siphoned from the humans at Abilene, he sent another party of Shadows both west and east of that facility, hoping to find them. With no bones or DNA evidence, it convinced him that the two humans were still alive, but just as elusive. Patience would prevail. Eventually he would find them and would become one step closer to destroying humanity.

Sooner came several hours later when unbeknownst to the trio, upon leaving Winema, an electronic relay registered at Porterhouse. The Shadows who had ventured southwest were in range to hear and followed the beacon. When the Shadows reached the perimeter of mountains, it stopped. Within the confines of Aeverless, Jonas traced the signal back to garage above the underground facility. He would send scouts to investigate, while he made his way to meet his minions in the mountains of southwest Texas. Leaving their underground facility, he could inspect the actual town of Aeverless. Twenty miles in diameter, the town's architect maximized the space wisely. The human had led them in through an entrance at the municipal building. The downtown area comprised a garage, bank, and municipal center. There was a park and opposite of it was the school, diner and department store, which also served as the major grocery store. Then there were 40 homes, the largest spanning three acres. Satisfied that they were all unoccupied, they continued heading out of town.

His team had just made their way out of town when the garage imploded sent fire balls in every direction. The fierce intensity of the flames took several hours to distinguish before he could survey the damage. The explosion turned the garage into a deep crater, severely damaging sections of the underground facility. Jonas surmised they had set off a trigger wire or detonator as part of the human's flimsy attempt of security. Summoning the minions to return from the mountains, he needed every able Shadow to repair the structure as quickly. Putting his fury aside, he would have to postpone his trip to the Texas Mountains. Jonas did not realize at that moment he made a tactical error when deciphering the relay. Built into the program was another sleeper, what past generations referred to as malware, that spread throughout the Shadows' equipment. Several hundred miles away, the entire scene is being recorded on old video equipment. Capturing the destruction of the garage and damage to the rebuilt facility, the sleeper went blank again, lying dormant, waiting for its next attack.

~

The vehicle came flying out of the ground, flying like a bat out of hell, smack into another furious storm. Visibility was horrendous. Debris was flying about them with winds howling over 70 miles an hour. The vehicle remained undeterred; however, with wheels spiked, and the front equipped with a razor like teeth, both demolishing everything in its path. From its hiding place, eyes watched with intensity as the vehicle came barreling out of the mountain. Moving with great speed, it leaves its dead carcass behind and makes its way into the compound before the door closes. Following the trail, it stops at the four entrances into the facility. Scaling the wall, it finds the fifth entrance and slithers inside and heads towards the main security console. Inputting a set of commands, it watches the interactions of the trio who spent several days there. Two girls and one guy. The resemblance between the two girls was familiar. Bayja and Brooks both had the Morrows smile and eyes. Alexander was much taller than his father Hennessey, but he exhibited features of the man on to another generation. Typing in another set of commands, he watches Jonas spinning his wheels, first at Aeverless. Extracting the small recorder from the floor panel, it settles down in the medical laboratory waiting to see what fun the trio has in store for him. The eyes wait for the Shadows and Jonas to arrive to this destination.

~

Onboard the vehicle, Bayja, Alex and Brooks sat glued to their seats, breathing, eyes wide open looking but they could not see a thing. The sky was as black as the terrain and all they could think and pray was they would make it out alive and intact. For over two hours, the vehicle battled the elements with its lights glowing in the dark. The vehicle increased its speed and barreled face first down what appeared to be a deep gorge. The embankment opens and shuts as the vehicle abruptly stops. A thick fog shrouded the vehicle. They were glad that they had not removed their protective gear. Sixty minutes passed before the fog disseminated. The console and screens became alive, informing its crew that they could now pull off their outer gear and move about. The speed slowed to a steady fifty miles an hour down the path. It slowed as it approached a large cave entrance. Snaking its way down the trail, the vehicle slows at the changed supercarrier, docked at the pier. Several drones surround the vehicle, inspecting it from head to toe. When they appeared satisfied, the vehicle starts up slowly down the pier and boards the waiting vessel. Large bay doors open, and the vehicle enters, shutting off its engines once reaching the bay lift, which secures the wheels in place. As the lift descends, an overhead speaker motioned its guests toward a bank of hatches. As they approached, the doors opened, and two gentlemen came forward. Recognizing them, Bayja speeds ahead, arms stretched wide for a hug.

 Aeverless 3_2

"Alex, Brooks," she smiles ear to ear, "meet the Cousins." Brooks, noncommittal, looked the two gentlemen over. Alex stepped up to the gentleman on his left; both men are dressed identical. The difference was the man on the left wore an old Yankees ball cap.

"I know you," he states. The gentleman nods in agreement. When Alex was nine, his family took in a stranger for a couple of weeks. His father claimed that the man was a fellow police officer visiting from the West Coast on his way to NewMaineland. He made quite an impression on the young Alex. First because of his stature, the man was well over six feet tall. Second, he found the man to be a wonderful storyteller. Prior to the last war, the man had travelled the world and spoke of exotic places, different cultures foods.

The two men turned their attention to Brooks. The shorter of the two, wearing a Dodgers shirt, spoke first. "Your father had moved you all out of New York, and Aeverless wasn't the place where you could just come and visit without people being suspicious. Yet, he knew you would need to recognize us when the time would come. So, I'd like to tell you a story about Argo and Hondo."

"Stop," Brooks cautions as she raises her hand. Talking to Dodger shirt she asks, "Do you have a scar that runs from your big toe to your ankle on the left side?"

"I do," he confirms.

"Then you must be Hondo." Turning to his companion she continues, "And you must be Argo." Both men smile in agreement and give both Brooks and Alex a big bear hug.

"It's good to see you, all grown up and well," Hondo starts. "Welcome to Aeverless 3_2. Let us get inside. We have a lot to catch up on and we need to leave while there's a break in the storm." All three of their guests looked at each other and then the Cousins perplexed. Hondo explained they would learn the origin of the vessel and its ties to the illustrious underground facility once they were out to sea, and asked Brooks to explain to her companions how she knew their names. They continue onto the elevator and make their way down several floors. While traveling Brooks explains her dad told her stories of what she thought were two fictional characters who traveled the world looking for adventure and building some incredible inventions along the way. Hondo and Argo interrupted as they passed points of interest on the carrier as they headed towards the main navigation room.

Secured at the helm, the carrier leaves the pier and slowly submerges. "I understand the break in the storm,

but why do we need a carrier to get to Guatemala."
"Well about that," as Argo turns to face them, "the plan
has changed. Another reason for the quick exit is this,"
as he turns his attention back to the TV monitor before
them. He pushes play and shows them the footage their
spy cam captured of the underground facility, the
progress and the well-timed sabotage on their part to
slow them down. "We've set some more booby traps
and don't want to be around if there are Shadow scouts
near Winema," Hondo chuckled. He said that the tunnel
brought them to the Oregon coastline and the Pacific
Ocean. Instead of heading southwest to South America,
they would make their way to some Alaskan islands.
Again, Alex questioned why. "Let's just say we're
following a hunch," Hondo interjects. "A lot of it
depends on what Brook remembers of her father's last
days, plus some footage from the original Aeverless,
Porterhouse, and Dugway. You all have seen none of
that footage yet, but you have time as we travel. Come,
the carrier is underway now and needs minimal
supervision. Let us give you the full tour of our home
for a while."

Taking the elevator back up several floors, they start at
the hangar. Besides the vessel that led them to the
Cousins, there were also several other utility vehicles,
tanks and construction like monstrosities used for
excavation and excursions. On the same floor was a
large quarantine and decontamination area.

"During the late 21st century, our country reconsiders where to send our most senior officials, along with supporting parties in business, healthcare, education and farming in case of a catastrophic event. Porterhouse was one of those locations on land. Aeverless, the underground facility, was the Trojan horse on land. It meant much of the technology and security remained mid-level until they detected the infected. When your father sealed you from his fate, we overwrote the systems at least to protect you. We could only watch some much from afar. Because you drew straws and stayed hunkered down there, we had to figure out another way to get you to us. It was us sending Alex to you. One misfortune that turned into a gem was the Shadows interception of the designator sent to Abilene," Argo conceded. They make their way to the massive kitchen and media area, where the group sits for a while.

"This vessel represents the real Aeverless bunker, at sea. When the Fathers formed, we nominated one individual that would be our Trojan horse. Brooks, we chose your father. In all our documents, except for your father, we erased our legal identities. In all our missions and correspondence, we never identified each other by our legal names. We used our nicknames only, mine being Hondo, and we even had a secondary name for your father. Within our inner circle, we knew him as Haven. There is one other piece of information I feel we need to disclose. Everything we planned for, every contingency, every mission was a guarded secret. Even then we included scenarios of what would we do in case of security breaches or complete technology failures. Central, your father elected to raise you by himself. When your father became a dad again, the plan was for one of us to raise your sister."

"Wait, what," Bayja stammers. Frowning, she becomes agitated and melancholy at the same time. All this time she thought she was alone to find out now that she has a sibling. Then, just as the thought came, it left her as she raised her head and studied Brooks more. Instinctively, Brooks did the same. Taking Brooks' hand, she reflects, "I remember this trip we took to South America when I was twelve. We stayed there a couple of months before moving on. Dad never repeated a place, but again when I was almost thirteen, we returned and stayed a couple of months like before. There was a woman who gave birth a few days before we returned the second time. I do not remember anyone saying what she had, but Dad left me with her, explaining that he had something important to do. You remind me of her. That same fiery spark and mane of hair."

"Close, but no," Argo informs them. "You both share the same father, but different mothers. You are correct though, that the woman he left you with is Brooks' mother. Your mother was a distant cousin of hers that lived in the States. Their similarities drew him to her." Brooks smiles. "I'm glad we're sisters. We have a lot to catch up on. Even though your father is my biological father, Daytona raised me as his own. I would like to think your father had a hand, though it was long distance." "Agree," Bayja murmurs, nodding, "and don't worry, I only see Alex as a brother. No intentions of sharing him with you." The three of them laugh as the Cousins get their meaning. "Okay," Argo says to no one in particular, "I guess we need to change the living quarter's arrangement." The conversation slows as they enjoy a meal together. The Cousins tell the trio that they have earned an extended break and to take the next few days just relaxing, getting their sea legs and reviewing the footage in the media room. They were free to roam around the carrier and familiarize themselves with every compartment and floor. Later that evening, as Alex and Brooks readied for bed, they reflected on the past few days. "So, our meeting wasn't fate after all," she teases. "I beg to differ," he responds. "Who knew that we would feel what we feel. That, this is destiny. Something tells me though that the Cousins will not complete this journey with us. They are only getting us to the next point. Why the islands off Alaska? From my understanding of history, and what we have seen of the maps prior to the last war, Alaska is underwater. Plus, we haven't found our father's lockers or the real meaning of Haven."

"I know," she agrees, "however I'm going to take your advice and for the next few days I just want to sleep, relax and visit our virtual beach on deck 6."

Down in the engine room, the Cousins mounted the two torpedo heads in the first two slots. The men equipped the carrier for twelve. They disguised these two and accessible from their quarters. Each pod slot contained food and weaponry for a few months for two individuals. There was a similar pod hidden in the room they placed Alex and Brooks, larger to accommodate up to six individuals with provisions for up to six months. They set the coordinates to deliver it to what they hoped was the Shadows' airship. The Cousins would be the bait leading the Shadows away from the trio's true destination. Time would come again that they would need to be honest with the trio, but for now the task was to prepare them all for what was to come.

~

Near the Washington coastline,

 As Aeverless 3.2 was leaving its safe harbor and making its way to the Alaskan islands, two Shadows were scouring the dead carcass they found near the Washington and Oregon coast. A faint murmur of engines reverberated through the low canyon area of their hideaway. Contacting the Dugway facility, it instructed them to investigate and report any findings.

Some thousand miles away, Jonas reached the outskirts of Quitman Mountains. Spreading his team out, they searched the terrain until reports filter in reporting visuals of housing posts spotted. One located some fifteen miles southwest of his location showed promise as initial reports confirmed a disturbance within the last month. Making their way, he noticed despite the density of green foliage, the surface was rocky. As he was the first successful fusion of human DNA and Shadow that lasted over one year and had working human faculties, he could distinguish some colors in the spectrum. He also could hide his feelings and thoughts from his cohorts, but still communicate telepathically. True Shadow lineage sees images of red or gray shapes, but their depth perception, like x-ray vision, is twice that of humans; Shadows can detect moving organs and veins. They stop as they spot a cabin on their horizon. Fanning, each dissect their portion of the structure. Jonas, intent on destroying every external building he finds, instructs them to destroy it. The fewer options the humans had, the better. Because the terrains and weather varied throughout the land, there would be certain buildings and facilities they would possess until they could create an environment underground where the Shadows could breed and thrive better.

In the remains, his eyes adjust, and he spots an odd shape pole with several indentions. He nears the apparatus and presses the first two buttons. Nothing happens. On the third the ground shakes and after several minutes, the cover gives way to a large circular steel lift. He becomes giddy in delight; could this be another underground facility? Motioning for two Shadows to stake patrol at the pole, the rest of his team stands on the lift. The fourth button shows no promise, but the fifth descends the lift into the earth. At

Aeverless 3.2, the media room picks up chatter and begins recording the descending lift into Porterhouse.

They ride in silence until the lift comes to a complete stop. Jonas orders his minions to investigate everything, leave no stone unturned but be careful not to destroy anything. He wants to be sure they record everything they find and add to their knowledge base for duplication and modification if needed. Jonas does not follow them into the cave, instead he waits for them to complete their investigation. He suspects that if this is indeed a human underground camp, there will be traps and other devices making them aware of intruders. Jonas turns and examines the lift; his mind searching through hundreds of records until he recognizes the contraption as a construction or industrial lift used in the late 20th, early 21st century. From this he gathers that either the government or business built and maintained it, as the lever to operate the lift was not recognizable. He cautions his troops to be on guard. A few hours pass before they give him all clear to proceed.

He makes his way down the cave, noting the temperature fluctuating until he reaches another wide opening. It surprises him at the differences between this location and their previous one, which has become their cloning base. Whereas the cloning location made use of artificial light, it encases this in steel and other minerals, this was an indoor replica of a small university campus underneath what could be a man-made mountain. Before him was a circular street with an outdoor park area, complete with living trees, plants and some type of concrete hole filled with water. Sitting on the opposite side of the street were five buildings; one long and rectangular, another octagon building, and two buildings connected by what appeared to be a walkway. He was right in his initial observation; this was man made and made to accommodate human living here. Interesting, he surmises. Interesting indeed. He swaps at his face as these little insects pop up out of the ground, being disturbed by their presence. Catching one in his palm, it resembles a gnat. He informs his team to lay a heavy mist of vapor that will clear the air of all pollutants. Within seconds the air was clear again. Jonas continued his walkthrough unaware he had made another critical mistake. Created by the fathers, the gnats collected samples of foreign matter to relay the information back to Aeverless 3.2 for interpretation.

The compound was pristine. Jonas and his team however where able to collect miniscule samples of a red, almost rust colored substance. Further examination uncovered that it was animal and human blood, another confirmation for Jonas that humans had indeed inhabited here. What puzzled him was why did they leave or were they planning on returning?

~

Brooks awakens with a start. Adjusting her eyes to her surroundings, she rises from the bed, leaving Alexander deep in slumber. She leaves the room and makes her way to the bridge where the Cousins are fiddling with some tools and gadgets laid out before them. Neither acknowledge her right away but sense she has entered their space. She makes her way to the front of the table, arms folded and eyes blazing for answers. "I feel we left something undone," she begins with her full focus on Argo's demeanor. "Why is it so important that I don't tell them about my dreams and that we've been communicating through them? And what was that thing in the woods at Winema?"

Both look up but only Argo answers. "What thing?" She describes the thing she saw in the woods before entering the compound and then again in her dreams. Some were recurring images she had at Aeverless, again at Quitman and new images of places she has never seen. Hondo instructs her to mention all but the new images to her sister and Alexander in the morning. "Your role and your survival will depend on you knowing when to share and when to keep solo council. Our responsibility is to make you a leader. ultimately you will learn to rely on your own instincts. Everything" he continues waving his arms in a circle around the room, "every scenario is speculative. In the end you will decide how to perceive, how to approach and the steps necessary to protect you and the others," Hondo explains. She sits and studies the gadgets before her. "What are these," she asks. "Let's talk about these later," Argo begins. "First, I need to tell you that story and maybe its best that you hear it first."

~

Alexander turns and finds himself alone in their quarters. He noticed Brooks has once again withdrawn into herself. As much as she puts up a brave front, he can sense when she is insecure or something or someone is stinking up her bullshit radar. Now he was not sure which it was as he felt he missed something of great significance before leaving Winema. Throughout their stay there he had the odd feeling that they were being stalked, not for prey but still the feeling was eerie none the less. He even thought things were out-of-place one evening when they returned from filling supplies. Alexander changes clothes and goes in search of Brooks finding her at the gym facility working the jab bag. She smiles as he enters, continuing to work the bag at a fevered pace. "You okay," he asks.

She stops, giving him another brilliant smile, "I'm okay." He watches her. Now realizing that he is not about to let the conversation go, she lets out a deep breath before saying what is weighing on her. "I wanted to wait until I spoke to you and Bayja together. While we were at Winema, I had the strangest dreams like we were being watched." Saying nothing, he sat and gave her time to explain further. She removes the boxing gloves and picks up the sketch book on the floor. Handing it to him, she replaces the gloves and resumes her workout as he thumbs through the pages. Finishing he states how impressed he is with the detail. "You drew all this today?" "No," she responded her breath as steady as her rhythm. "I drew a few in the tunnels at Winema while the vision was still fresh in my mind. I do not know if its fear of the Shadows creeping in as we head off into this unknown," "waving her hands in the air. "Whatever the case this feels real. I don't get the intent that this one doesn't want to hurt us, more like protect us."

Alexander studies the sketches closely. The eyes are similar yet different. Whereas the leader at Aeverless had almost a demonic look, these eyes have a determined yet haunted look about them. "Will you let me know when you have another dream?" his response soft, unchanged. She nods in agreement. "Anything else," he whispers as he grabs the bag, stopping her momentum, requiring her complete attention. She sees the worry in his face, the concern. Removing the gloves again, she motions him to sit. Sitting down in front of him she reassures him all is well. "Please trust me," she continues, "that when the time comes, I will reveal more."

"So, there is more," Alexander prods?

"You asked me to trust you unconditional. I have and I still do. I am asking you now to do the same. When the time comes, you will be glad you did."

~

From the door Bayja watches in silence. Without entering she turns and makes her way to the navigation center where Argo is working on some new contraption. "Secrets have a way of destroying trust," she begins.

"True," he answers not looking up from his work, "but each of you have a part to play. And that part must be instantaneous. Given time to think about it will make you think wrong. We did and it cost us your father and Daytona. I trust you all will do what is necessary when its necessary. This relationship between Alexander and Brooks, just how strong is it," looking up from his work cautiously eyeing her.

The two of them stare down the other for a few minutes. Bayja, wondering just what else they have not been told, lets it go for the moment and concentrates on her answer. "They have become quite close. I believe both would give their life for the other without hesitation. But whatever this is that we are still not privy to, I hope it does not build dams we cannot cross. I'll leave you to your work," she replies turning from the room and heads back down the corridor. Argo sets his tools down on the table and rubs his eyes. Seeing the three of them together brought back some memories he thought he long buried. Jonas, Jacob and Morrows Strangelove, fraternal triplets, the mad man, the cynic and the optimist.

Jonas, a psychopath, is the vilest of the three. Had he any inkling about having not one but two brothers, he would have bent hell into thousands of pieces to ensure he was the only remaining Strangelove. His father, a warped man, kept Jonas and gave what he considered the weaklings up for adoption. Turns out each brother was intelligent and quite fit. Morrows was the smartest of the group. That spoke volumes seeing that every member of The Fathers had an IQ of over 150. His thoughts turned back to the brothers. Jacob and Morrows favored each other while Jonas, did not resemble anyone in the immediate Strangelove bloodline. They had made the discovery when each of the brothers were being recruited to serve their country. Morrows, the first was lucky to have the records scrubbed but kept tabs on the two from a distance. After delving further into their history, he discovered Jonas resembled a distant uncle from the 20th century that was diagnosed as insane. It was not until the Dugway mission that they realized Jacob also had knowledge of his brothers. It is Jacob now that has him concerned. Somehow the virus infected two of the three brothers. Jonas has transformed and to their knowledge cannot shape shift like his brother Jacob. Jacob roams the area between Dugway and Winema like a bloodhound but has yet to strike. Brooks dreams has confirmed it, meaning it was imperative they get to the island quickly after sending the trio on their way. With the Shadows not aware of the advancements the government made, the trio should be able to use it to their full advantage changing the course of humans's history. That and Morrow's promise. Under no circumstances would his daughters ever know their direct relationship to Jonas, Jacob and the Strangelove family.

Jacob watches his narrow-minded brother Jonas pilfering through the remains at Porterhouse. The cameras had come online once the trio left, leaving neither him nor his brother any active accounts of trios' time there. Good move on Morrows part to make the changes after invading Dugway. No one would have suspected that we hide cameras some two thousand feet up in the atrium of Porterhouse. Well played to the Fathers. He suspected Jonas would not find much useful, only the tidbit that would lead him west here to Winema and their inevitable encounter. His thoughts turned to his nieces. Although he had not been near the tunnels when they departed, he could still sense their presence. Only Brooks could get a visual through her dreams, but no connection. Somehow Morrows had found a solution to that as well. Jonas' issue was that he did not factor that fancy suit would have deployed the DNA of the Shadows to other compatible donors. Fancy suit also knew of the Strangelove triplets. Unbeknownst to Morrows, he became infected during the mission at Dugway. Jacob could follow his brother's tracks for a while. Though Morrows could connect the dots, they planned to keep both daughters safe and unknowing about the other until came. He could handle Bayja. It was Brooks that gave him the greatest cause. She was unreadable. In his book anyone that visible yet invisible was a great threat. The day he entered the tunnels undetected, from a distance he watched her. Somehow though her body must have detected him as she disappeared without a trace. From the camera at the dock, he could see her, but once she boarded the ship, all traces of her disappeared again. He wondered how she would respond knowing that a snippet of Shadow DNA ran through her veins. How were they able to disguise it so well? And how was she infected before any of them? Is she even aware that she has Shadows DNA running through her veins? He discovered that tidbit from his only meeting with Morrows on the fateful day back at Dugway. There is nothing left for him to do now but sit, watch and wait for the Shadows to come.

~

Bayja, Alex and Brooks met on deck nine in the small mechanic room. It was one of four spaces free of cameras or mics. For added caution they spoke in the sign language Brooks taught them before leaving Winema. Brooks relayed the information she received from the Cousins and their theory that pieces of the Shadows air technology remained hidden somewhere between the Aleutian Islands and the Bering Sea. It was at Winema they discovered the anomaly in Brooks bloodwork. The horror that the gene has laid dormant for many years terrifies Brooks. When the time came for Alex and or Bayja to end her, she knew they would do so without hesitation. Her sister and Alex were working scouring Daytona's records in hope of a miracle. Somehow, he could work among them without being infected. Bayja also knew her father did as well, and somewhere there was a clue how they did it.

With her drawing of the Shadow at Winema complete, the group worked on making the Shadows presence known and detectable to Bayja and Alex. There would be no way to it without being in proximity. Still, anything was better than nothing at all and the closest test case to them was Brooks, the elephant in the room. Should they test her, and would it cause more damage than good? They deferred and keep at their plan—stay the course and follow their instincts. With the extra hands-on deck, the Cousins had assigned them general duties, to familiarize them with the ship, to learn new trades and to keep them from asking questions. Despite being several hundred feet underwater, the Cousins cautioned them to stay alert and weapon ready. The ship had sat open until ready for use. Despite all security cautions it was best to leave nothing to chance. They made their way down to the lower level when the bands on their wrists began illuminating bright red. Pulling out their radar gun, they realize they are not alone. Fanning out they tiptoe down the corridor, two front, one rear searching each room until the Cousins reach them midway. No one made a sound, moving in stealth mode as to not alert their uninvited guest. the closer they got to their prey; Brooks internal alarm system went haywire. She taps the Cousins, pointing for them to move behind her and stay at least 10 feet back, weapons ready on her command. On cue each tapped the gas mask which covered their face as the radon gas seeped from the ventilation system. There it was, visible only to the trio; an opaque skeleton that morphed from human form to its natural state, a body resembling nothing they had ever seen before. Its head, odd had gills of a fish covered by a prickly texture like a porcupine. The skull and eyes, like those of the ape and human family were large and protruded and had a weird covering like a snake, that could shed as it grows. The body, arms and legs long with razor like claws. A sight that known would soon forget. As the Shadow swung its arm to infect Bayja, Brooks total invisible stepped between them and gutted it like a fish. A green substance oozed to the floor, the gas burning it like acid. Alex motioned that the second was closing fast behind the Cousins. With lighting speed, Brooks took up flank and caught the Shadow by complete surprise. Now behind it, she snaps its spine and punctures the thick skin allowing the gas to eat at the tissues and thick green liquid vaporize. Staying in their protective gear, they again run the security protocols and run a deeper security check of all levels, not leaving any surface untouched. Not a word spoken between any for several hours, as they scrubbed and disinfected every particle ensuring their safety. Returning to navigation, each enter exhausted and tempers flaring.

"Explain," Bayja eyes full of anger and disbelief. "How did every detection we have in place, miss two Shadows? How was it possible" Alex and Brooks, stoned face, waited for an answer from the Cousins? Before Hondo could respond, Brooks silenced the group again, directing each to a neutral spot. They watch in silence as the third Shadow enters the space. Brooks motions for the group to resume their conversation. Hondo begins with having to leave the ship alone for several days, weeks at a time. They had hoped that the measures they had in place would suffice, as it was dangerous to board the ship. In doing so, would raise suspicion among the Shadows and defeat their true mission now. On cue, the hatches open to dispose of the waste. All three pods released from their bay, with two continuing southwards down the Pacific coastline, and the third diving deeper and heading towards the Bering Sea at lightning speed. The Shadow sits at the controls confused as the group has projected an image of themselves. The intercom system activates to play their conversation. It would need to scour the ship again to find their whereabouts; now it was solo and did not have help of his companions. It looks down at the panel and notices a counter counting down, 00:00:10; 00:00:09. Unbothered it rises and heads out of navigation to find the humans. Counter hits 00:00:00. Exhaust turns on full blast pumping radon into every crevice of the ship. The Shadow did not return to its hiding spot. It died instant. From the leading solo pod Hondo wishes his companions "God speed" and signs off. So far, their plan is working. From the docks prior to boarding the Cousins warned the trio of the possibility of Shadows on board. Quickly and quietly, they worked together to plot leading the Shadows off course while the trio continued. All were aware of the slight subtleties not only in Brooks DNA, but the markers in Bayja and Alex as well. The plan was to convince any listening devices that only Brooks stood out. It surprised the Cousins to learn that the trio did indeed know about Jonas and Jacob Strangelove. They ponder about how much to tell them about Morrows, but in the end, they departed with the information now knowing every advantage they could give them, they would need.

QUITMAN MOUNTAINS

Jonas stood on the platform where the train had departed from. Despite the efforts of the trio to cover their tracks, they are unaware of the small recording device Argo, the AI, leaves at the Cousins request. While watching the video he received word that a team of searchers near the Oregon coast found an entrance to an underground tunnel that showed signs of human activity. What a coincidence he thought as the map showed a direct path from here to the Oregon coast. Another interesting turn of events; it shows only the man from the previous facility entering the train. No sightings again of the young woman who assisted him. Strange feeling in his gut; to pursue this lead. He was sure, no adamant, that the young man and woman were key to their, his success. His problem now was getting as many as comrades or awakening on the way to this Oregon place. He motioned for them to spread out, each taking a different route from the train depot. As much as he cautioned to look for traps, they encountered many and the casualties were high. His problems intensified once he reached the desert. The terrain and temperatures were not conducive to their skeletal structure and the underground shelter limited. Whatever means his prey used to reach this place, he was undeterred. Just as he had encountered problems, he assumed they did as well and are vulnerable leaving him victorious in their capture. Jonas continued to press, picking up Shadows on his way, not stopping pushing forward at a tremendous pace. Strangelove was salivating. Jonas could feel the end near. Adrenaline pumping, they continued and within a few days reached the outskirts of Winema National Forest. Hoping for a change in the terrain and conditions, he became aggravated. The further north he went, the worse the terrain and weather became. He suspected that once they could comb the forest thoroughly, he would have many choices of underground safety. The operative word however was safety. From his viewpoint the forest reminded him of a black hole; deep, murky and no end in sight. It did not help that the ground cover was hardened black ice, and with no light being able to penetrate through the deep trees and mist, the footing was treacherous. At the entrance he made the search parties smaller, only four each spanning out a thirty-degree radius from each other. It took them a complete day just to travel three miles. On the third day he struck gold in finding an entrance to an old mining tunnel. Calling the other parties back to his location, they began making their way underground.

From his vantage point Jacob watched with great curiosity. His brother, despite his scholarly knowledge, was an idiot. His drive to conquer left little room for planning any defensive moves. Jacob calculated it would be another hour or more before his brother and goons would make it to the fork in the road. He had disabled all but a few of the security precautions. Jacob needed his brother here, intact and one piece where he could deliver the critical blow himself. Yes, this should be an interesting meeting indeed.

~

At the northern tip of Winema, far below the surface, another pair of eyes watched with great intent. The perfect cocktail of radon, remnants of ethanol and nuclear waste made his hiding place off limits to everyone, including his comrades Argo and Hondo. He spent years making the right arsenal of protective gear, he placed in the trio's pod. They would need it the further west into the Bering Sea they traveled. Morrows glances at his hidden cameras. Like clockwork everything was going according to his plans. He knew he set the perfect trap; one in which he will give his life for it to succeed. He watched his brothers, the idiotic psychopath and the checker player. For his girls to advance, he would need to return from the grave for this family reunion. Keeping his identity hidden from the Fathers was the hardest, most difficult thing he ever had to do besides having Dakota raise his youngest daughter. Morrows had to make his demise believable to set this current stage. He again thought of the two men on the screens in front of him. One despised everything in life and had every intent on ruling the world. The other, with some convincing would protect his daughters with his dying breath. He had to make him a believer. Both he and Jacob had spent the better part of six years here hidden. Once a beautiful place, this Oregon was dense beyond measure and dangerous for all who dare enter. One reason, they, the Fathers, chose this as their command post was the terrain. In the history books, Oregon's ecosystem was remarkable; filled with volcanoes and an abundance of lakes and forests, it was perfect for agriculture and technology to coexist. Scientists and meteorologists baffled at the changing climate worldwide could not explain the handful of areas like the likes of Oregon. Oregon was a true enigma. Extremes of cold and heavy fog, it was a wonder that the underbrush of the forest and volcano activity still existed. Yet it thrived in a frightening capacity. Most of the shadows that ventured into this region stayed close to the Pacific shore. He watched as Jonas and his minions dwindled in numbers until, they reached the underground bunker. It was imperative that during this strike only Jonas remains alive. Leaving any of the true form Shadows alive would allow them the ability to procreate and that was the last thing they needed. That and a long-drawn-out family reunion with Jonas.

~

He remembered his first encounter with Jacob. Both learning simultaneously that from one embryo, three fraternal brothers created. Known as Jeremiah, growing up in New California, he thought nothing special of his childhood, though most would disagree. His parents, wealthy, spent their days and years traveling the world. Until he started school, he had traveled with them to exotic places, each experience was to know the town as a local–not as a tourist. Education and knowledge to them equated power. Power to give back and see the world as it is, a devout admirer of people and things. Around the time he started his formal education, his parents had informed him they had adopted him. They had found him abandoned on their door. It was them who had helped him find out about his natural birth parents. It was not until later that he learned about the forged documents and his actual identity obscure from him until joining the agency. Despite wanting to shield him from the world, instead they helped shape and define a young man of culture, compassion and honor. It was his adolescent years that went amuck starting with his introduction to Jacob. Looking back on the memory now, he knows it was not accidental. Nothing about his brothers or their method was accidental or even coincidental. Everything they did was logical, another notch to their endgame. Entering his biophysics class in college–becoming curious after his mother developed a muscular deficiency some years ago–he sat down and struck a conversation with a young man seated next to him. They became fast friends and as the days went by, Morrows sensed something quite odd but fascinating about him. They seem to complete each other's thoughts and could sense physical and intellectual patterns in each other. Though Morrows considered himself an open book, he found himself guarded around Jacob. Best buddies yes, but something peculiar nagged at Morrows about Jacob's demeanor. Just something under the surface that one would get a glance of every now and again. With it came an uneasy feeling, ominous and sickening at the same time. Enough to make one's skin crawl and then the next moment he made one feel at complete ease. His parents told warned him about folks like that. They are the ones that would slit your neck without hesitation, right in front of you while singing your praises. Even the recruiters interviewing candidates for the agency, informed him that his DNA markers were a match to Jacob's. He almost missed the cut because the agency thought he had falsified information. Only when they investigated further, they found both men were honest on their applications. Morrows, the calmer and saner of the two, trained and joined the elusive club known as The Fathers. It was then he learned just how cold and callous Jacob was. Although he could never prove it, he felt Jacob played a role in the death of his parents.

It was during his first weeks at Aeverless where he discovered his passion for security and learned of his other brother Jonas. Each of the recruits spent some time there, with Daytona being the last. It was no accident that Daytona selected Aeverless as his last tour of duty. It was a way for him to mix among the locals, learn and raise his daughter with no suspicion to her true heritage. There Morrows and the others knew they could instill and do the most damage to the suit man and his minions, Jonas, stationed at Dugway. Jonas had been on the agency's watch list for quite some time; not only for his intelligence but lack of compassion and human decency made him a suspicious target to perpetrate heinous crimes against anyone who crossed him wrong. He was power hungry, even as a kid, and would position himself with any and everyone who would help further his cause. Morrows watched him now on the screen scurrying around like a ferret looking for its next meal. Winema South, as maps referred to it, disinfected after the trio's visit both by him and Jacob was ready to greet him. He had just missed Jacob at the site which was a good thing. He did not want the encounter until all three were present. With the trap set, he was about to get his wish within the next few days. The thing about his latest cocktail that he loved the most was that it was unexpected - undetectable until moments before one's vital organs shut down. As Jonas has more human features, the toxin would take longer to work on him. It would render his puppet of followers immobile within another twenty-four hours. They will be useless, unable to defend and unable to reproduce which is what Morrows needed. The more vulnerable Jonas becomes the better chances his daughters and Alex would have to make it to the next facility, under radar and undetected. He would have to time the meeting right as he would not get another opportunity to bring his brothers together. It was to be his last living moment, and he had to make the count.

The hours dwindled down in a slow crawl; Morrows conserved his energy. As predicted the minions did not know what was happening to their bodies and Jonas, weak from the toxic atmosphere was helpless to retreat or even send for help. They entered Winema, Morrows closed the entrances like a Venus fly trap; even Jacob in his hidden cocoon above the health unit could not escape back into the tunnels leading out of Winema through the mine shafts. He did not know what the effects of the next toxins had on Jacob, but he could tell they slowed his movements. He waited another twelve hours before leaving his shelter. From his fortress Morrows set the charges to blow and obliterate everything in fifteen-mile radius thirteen hours from now. Making his way into the last open entrance, he sealed it shut behind him and made his way through the last open mine shaft, leaving traces of the toxin behind him. The skeletal remains of his brother's army covered the ground, permeating an indescribable stench. Using his blowtorch, he sprayed the walls and ground and watched the remains fizzle to dust. He thought of every detail knowing that the more time he gave Brooks, the better. Following his pre-determined path, he allows the last toxins to infect him as he enters the security area from a hidden panel in the infirmary. Sensing another presence, Jacob also leaves his refuge and makes his way to the security center.

Sitting in the security center, Jonas tries to make sense of the system before him. Weak from the toxins, he realizes his tactical error. It would be weeks before another team of Shadows made their way to Oregon and work their way through the frozen terrain, hopeful that they would have a trail to follow. He was going to be resourceful and find, not only food, but a way to remove the toxins from his body. One thing he knew for certain; there were other humans at play here. He did not think that Bayja and the two people traveling with her had enough gumption, much fewer skills to prepare a trap this elaborate. Whoever was helping them, had months maybe even years to make this a formidable prison. It confirmed his worst fears after a few hours that it confined him in hell. And in his current physical condition, he struggled to think and find an exit strategy. Although he was in a weaken state and it blurred his vision, his other senses alerted him he was no longer alone. A human and something else sinister were nearby. Food he thought. He darted around the space as fast as he could, looking for anything he could use as a weapon or at least give him an advantage. "Getting sloppy in your old age Jonas" a voice rumbled from behind him. Impossible! He turns and finds Morrows standing with a sly grin pasted on his face. "Our brother" as Morrows moves closer, closing the space in between them, "should join us momentarily."

"Brother," Jonas choked. It shocked both that Jonas could still speak as he had not had a need to in over six years. "Ah, family reunion. How nice of you Morrows to plan this event, but I am afraid it is a little too late to make nice and be brothers," Jacob interrupts as he studies the elusive Jonas Strangelove in person. Making full eye contact he continues. "Jonas, you're not quite what I expected. But then again, we should have met before you decided you enjoyed fusing human DNA with whatever damn creature has been inhabiting our world for the last hundred years. You are indeed brilliant and also profusely insane."

Jonas retreats, backing until his body contacts a chair at the console behind him. He sits and for the first time in many years astonished at the sight before him. Brothers? What started as a snark became a snorkel and he laughed, incredulous to the sight before him. His eyes darting from Morrows to Jacob and then back again to his memory; of the man and the body he encompassed before the transition and fusing of molecules took place. "Since I am forced to speak, I'll allow Morrows to explain this impromptu reunion before I devour both of you. And while you are explaining, who are these humans you are protecting? Now that I see you, I know it was you and that gangly group, so-called Fathers, who have been helping them. Are you all alive, or just a few with the rest helping from their graves?" he asked.

It was Jacob however who responded. "Morrows you are a sly devil. Despite our differences I believe I understand your plan. Let us see how long it takes

Jonas before he connects the dots. You were right all those years ago. Had we met as young boys, I believe both Jonas and I would have made different choices. That is all in hindsight. We must deal with the here and now. As I promised Morrows then, I will keep my word and do whatever is necessary. So, dear brother Jonas, the ball is now back in your court with no explanation from us. This, the two of us is all you are getting. So, Mr. Genius, or so you say, do you not know what's happening here" Morrows moves closer to Jonas and in passing hands his brother Jacob an old stopwatch. It pings as he clasps it in his hands. Slow to react, Jonas moves, knowing he needs to make a play to diffuse one man quickly. "Godspeed Jacob," Morrows whispers as he pulls the gun from his pocket. Before either brother could respond, he puts the barrel to his left ear and pulled the trigger. "NO," Jonas screams, startled and unprepared for the chain of events. Jacob pulls the pin from the watch as he spins and exits from the direction he came from. "Until we meet again, brother," he laughs at Jonas as the last of the toxin seeps into the room, clouding the air like a San Francisco morning fog, allowing him to escape from Jonas' grasp.

This last gas was different as Jonas can breathe, yet the gas renders him immobile, unable to move. Even he had to applaud Morrows, for he knew that the first move Jonas would make would be to feed, instead of following the man called Jacob. With his sight distorted, all he could rely on was his hearing. He had heard of Jacob, but every scrap of intel he received did not have one photograph of the man. He could only assume that either Jacob or Morrows cleaned this from the databases. No need to spend energy on the inevitable moment. He slows his vitals and waits until he can move. He would feed, and then he would wait for reinforcements to appear. Then he would start again, back at the beginning and his first encounter with Morrows. Interesting indeed, being one of three born from the same egg. Morrows, Jacob and Jonas. Yes, he would start back at the beginning, determined not to repeat the same mistake again. With Morrows delivering the fatal blow by a bullet to his brain, he cannot recover or abstract any information that would be vital to why one or both determined to help that bothersome trio. Now more than ever he was quite certain that the young woman traveling with Bayja and the man name Alex was the key. Yes, whoever she is, she is vital to his plans of dominating the world.

As Jacob returns to the mine shaft, he notices that the watch his brother gave him was an old-fashion compass. Following the trail outlined before him, he picks up his pace, determined to put as much distance between him and Jonas as he can. He takes over two hours to reach the exit. The temperature, well below freezing, prompts him to pick up the backup and add more layers. The sky, always dark, grumbled with lightening, a sign that another storm was rapidly approaching. He spots a monster truck about a hundred and fifty feet from his location. Scanning his surroundings, he does not detect any danger and makes his way to the truck. He enters and sees that his brother had indeed left him an exit strategy. Upon his entry the GPS chimed, scans his retina and hands, identifying him as Jacob Strangelove. The truck starts and begins plowing through tundra at a moderate rate of speed; lights off. Fastening his seatbelt, his chair he notices is flexible, able to move not only sideways but turn a full one hundred and eighty degrees, allowing him sight from any direction. He sees another care package of food, clothing, and other essentials stored in the cabin behind him. This was Morrows doing. His brother never ceased to amaze him.

"Welcome Jacob," the voice familiar was that of his deceased brother. "Our plan, I trust, will buy the girls more time. Glad to see that Whitehouse joined them. I have already entered the coordinates to your next location. The good news is that it will take Jonas at least a good six months to a year to pick up your trail. He will want to find you first. The bad news. He will recover some data at Winema South that I could not destroy. He will discover Brooks' identity and who she is. As much as I wanted to keep her and Bayja from learning about Jonas, I could not do so. Maybe that is for the best that they know everything. Whatever they do from this point on, they are on their own. About a day's travel from here, the Cousins should arrive at the designated rendezvous point where you will change vehicles. From there, it should take you about another week to reach our home base. If the trio is successful in reaching the outer perimeter of their next location, their vehicle will emit a signal to you before self-destructing. Good luck, brother." The cabin became silent as Jacob reflected on his brother. He was glad for the time they could reconnect and put to rest all the uneasiness between them. As the truck was navigating itself, he made himself comfortable and closed his eyes. No telling when he would sleep like this again.

Ground Zero

The trio sat in silence before the lone window, giving them a glimpse of the murky ocean before them. They maneuvered through the blocks of ice and debris collected from years of shifting volcanic lines, tsunamis and earthquakes. They were three days into their journey, none having a clue where they are heading next. The only thing from keeping them from going stir-crazy was the provisions onboard. Everything was a throwback from a century ago; several hardback books, a CD, DVD player and television with an array of movies and albums from the late 20th and early 21st century. The gear, scuba diving equipment, wet suits tailored to increase or remove padding based on the temperature and other outside elements. Walkie-talkies, hand-held radios, and digital and old fashion compasses. They expect the unexpected, so they put little thought into why these items would be necessary. It was day seven that everything came into perspective. While discussing the movie selection for the evening, Bayja picked up two movies, a comedy, and a meaningless action film. Once the films started playing, however, they realized the markings are incorrect. The first film entitled Ground Zero, part fact and part theory, based on two strange meteor landings or sightings in 2190 and 2211. They reported the first to have occurred on the Diomede Islands in 2190, while Dugway Utah recorded the second in 2211. It was interesting to note that a scientist named Strangelove was part of the initial recovery tea. Theory or rumor at the time was the meteors were an alien race evading Earth, and they had infiltrated humans. The second film, Truth, was a recording made by Morrow outlining the Strangelove family and their direct involvement with both meteor landings, along with testing for alien DNA with volunteers and unsuspecting Americans. He talked in great length about his adoption and discovering his relationship to the Strangelove's, along with two other brothers, Jacob and Jonas. Another fact coming to light, they were all born on the same day. It was important to note that he and Jacob were identical twins, while Jonas had a very distinct look and personality. Like their father, Jonas was a true sociopath. He marveled at the fact that their father separated them at birth. How could anyone make such a choice? In retrospect, he was thankful. That choice saved both his and Jacob's lives.

"He must have spent years collecting these items," Alexander pondered. "Thoughts," he said, speaking to both sisters who remained quiet. In such a short time, he knew their moods and the one in the room now was to leave them alone. Kissing Brooks on the forehead, he rises from the sofa and leaves the room. Neither sister spoke for a time, the silence telling with only the hum of the engine and their own thoughts racing through their minds. After several minutes, scraping the floor with her chair, Bayja rises and taps Brooks on the shoulder, motioning her to follow. They find Alex tinkering with an old radio in the mechanics area. Speaking to no one, Bayja starts, "Why go backgrounds? I mean, with all the technology and advancements made, why invent items from the 19th and 20th century?"

"I think I found the answer," Alex responds while holding up the radio. "On first inspection, they look like replicates, but they are updates and we have the blueprints. Ground Zero is the reason. The second wave of aliens quickly adapted to our technology. That was the major reason the Fathers wrote code to destroy the Argo, and each vehicle we have used since, along with the navigation, has been more archaic. In a couple of boxes," he states pointing to the storage area in the cabinets behind him, "I found these rough drafts." He explains the radios and how to use their frequency. "Wherever we are going," he cautions, "it will test our skills. The gauge shows we are about another day or so from our destination. I suggest we get a couple hours of sleep before we pack up our remaining gear."

"Let's pack now," Brooks suggests. "Although the Cousins eluded the Shadows were among us on the last vehicle, it left us on edge. I would rather be prepared to get off this vessel and keep moving, alert than running on half empty."

Agreeing, they moved swiftly, packing their necessities in the station wagon they found encompassed in a lone containment hull. During the 20th century, they referred this vehicle to as a recreation vehicle, or RV. They reinforced the total body of the vehicle from the frame to the windows. Completely tinted from the outside, nothing could view the interior. The windows reinforced to protect from any type of ammunition and immune from every heat seeking or thermal detection source. Driver and passenger seats turned a full 180 degrees. There was a small kitchen, bedroom with bath and an open area with two comfortable lounges to eat or work. Next to the refrigerator was a door which allow access to the lower level where they found extra fuel, camping equipment, ammunition and guns. They needed no vote. After loading the last box with the DVD's, DVD player, blueprints and diving equipment, they fastened themselves in. In console in between the driver and passenger seat, they found a set of journals, only listing a series of coordinates. Placing it back in the console, they rest. The gauge now read less than nine hours before reaching their new destination.

About eighteen hours away, a lone shadow travels at a snail's pace on the ocean floor. The acid from the mangled coral eats and cuts at his skin, leaving his organs and circuitry exposed to the water filled with salt, freezing temperatures and black molded fungi, as dark as tar. If his body allowed him, he would follow the faint murmur of the ship that continued northwest from the Washington coast. Unlike his comrades that died aboard the larger vessel when it blew up, he had been attempting to compromise the outside hull of the vessel now travelling west, without success. Before being blown clear of the smaller vessel, he detected three bodies inside. He would follow and report back to Leader. Yes, our leader will be pleased.

Two hours into their slumber, the engines on the RV revved up. Startled by the sound, they awaken to see the vehicle unfold a protective covering, like the diving gear they had onboard. The tires had inflated to become floatation device. After covering the RV and tires secured in place, the flooring beneath the vehicle moves upward. The hatches above the RV opens, releasing the RV as it moves at a sped-up pace, propelling them upwards, breaking the plane of the ocean, sitting them on the frozen ground. The engines increase their speed, moving them closer to what appeared to be an island in the middle of nowhere. On cue, the navigation system lights up. Pulling out the journal, they set course to the first set of coordinates designated Aeverless three dot zero. Below the ice, the vessel turns south and moving back towards the lone shadow, still a day's travel away. Jacob has met up with the Cousins. They are finishing their last lines of defense while waiting for Jacob, who is still recuperating and waiting for reinforcements. Several hours past. The lone shadow sees the vessel moving in slow motion, twenty kilometers to the southwest. Ice has formed on the structure; the shadow intrigued, knowing his prey vulnerable. His outer form has had time to adjust to the cold, making it a little more bearable to maneuver. Just as he reaches the stern, the vessel explodes sending shards of glass and gas everywhere. The shadow never knew what hit him as his outer form and circuitry bubbled and disintegrated into a blueish black oily substance. At the outpost, a single chime signal Jacob and the Cousins. Nodding to each other, they acknowledge their last line of communication to the trio is severed. "God speed," Jacob whispers hoping the best for his nieces and humanity. At the old mine shaft Jonas reels that the gift his brother and the mysterious young girl had left behind. Watching the video screen, he gets his first full view of the young troublemakers as children. He recognizes the male as a youthful version of one of the Fathers and the older girl as Bayja. The younger slimmer girl was darker than Bayja and had a head full of curly hair and kept her face obscure from the screen. It was not until the last ten minutes of the tape that he caught a full composite of her. The footage, new, maybe only a few weeks at most was crisp; every detail sharp and in tune. Looking into the camera she fired a direct shot. "Uncle Jonas," she chirped with a devilish smile on her face, "they have not introduced us. My name is Brooks, the daughter of Morrows and Haleya." His mind wandered for a split second to the only woman he had ever loved, and he wondered if this child was his and not his brother's. The laughter returned his attention to the film. "You are a formidable opponent, but for now I must declare checkmate. Reinforcements, your disciples will not be coming soon. The trail to you I am afraid is a big mess. We have taken extra precautions so it might be six months, maybe a year before they find you. We left you with a few rations. One day we will meet. I am certain of it. But until then, catch us if you can" The film then disintegrates, sizzling and bubbling like someone took a handful of baking soda and dropped into a vial of vinegar. "No," he screams. His echoes landing on only his ears and the surrounding walls. In his weaken state he heads down the corridor of the medical unit only to find it caved in, along with the two smaller rooms on the left of the main control room. The entrance also caved in, one hundred and fifty feet, give or take a couple. Somehow air was still being filtered in. He just needed to rest, regain his strength and he would figure it out. Clever of her indeed. No landmarks or clues where the video originated from and destroying it once viewed now limits his ability to pick up on anything else. Clever of his brothers too leaving him limited in mobility and without reserves to do his bidding. He did not believe for one second it would take is troops six months to find him. This trio had bested him again. It took eight months and seventeen days, and, in their efforts, they had failed him. Miserably. No signs of Jacob or the trio. They had vanished. Even the lone signal that they had received from the sea was silent. To follow that lead would take him another six months at least to find adequate transportation and modifications to the vessel. The fathers planned well. They left nothing to chance and no substance materials to use in this waste. This time out he would be more strategic. The repair work at the Aeverless site was taking longer than he expected. Here in the old mine shafts, he could make them useful. It would take time. He could not afford another fiasco that would cost him the capture of the human's last great hope. No, he would stay here for the time being and make this an impenetrable fortress. Sending teams out to the north and advancing a hidden cell southwest from here to check the shorelines would be his best bet in finding his brother and the trio. He was certain that they took separate paths. The last transmissions of the team investigating the lighthouse confirmed this was the trio had gone to sea. That would have been his play; an advantage indeed. Making an opponent exert more energy. The transmissions ended about four to six hundred miles offshore. No matter, we outnumbered them. He would lose a few soldiers, but the loss would allow him to make necessary adjustments to survive in the most brutal conditions and temperatures. With any operation, soon or later, costly mistakes will allow him to capitalize on. They would need a few more months to develop underwater transportation. He would stay restrained, show patience and continue to inspect, reinspect every piece of information to their whereabouts. From all indications, the frozen underworld would be hard to survive for more than a couple of months. Wherever they landed, Confident he would find them. He delighted in knowing their slaughter would be brutal and swift.

The New Colony

The RV, and its occupants, traveled on the frozen surface for another three hours before the surface changed again to warmer water. Submerging to the ocean floor, they continued their charted course northwest before reaching a cavern opening. The RV stops, turning off all exterior lights and the engines before entering the opening, which clamored behind them. The RV sputters on for another hour before the water changed from total ebony to a shade of deep blue. From their seats, it amazed the trio at the scenery that surrounded them. Coral, underwater plants and things with gills are swimming about like they didn't have a care in the world. They continued, the water getting shallow, seeing blue sky, trees and a shoreline before them. The RV transforms once more from being a water raft to a land vehicle making its way ashore. The contrast was extraordinary. Instead of the thick foggy atmosphere of Winema, the foliage was green with the sun filtering through the treetops that seemed to stretch over twenty feet in the air. As the vehicle continued inward at a snail's crawl, there were still patches of sun carving through, making the path ahead of them presentable. The shrubbery splashed colors of purple, yellow and orange, with the ground covering altering between mossy grass and mounds of damp red clay. They speculated amongst themselves that it had recently rained. About ten miles in, the heavens opened to a torrential rain shower. The RV slowed even further while sheets of water poured viciously, not allowing the wiper blades to keep up. Visibility became nil and they could not see a thing. The RV continued onward, following the course already chartered.

From the watchtower, a group of individuals watch as the RV maneuver through the underbrush. Prior to making land, the undercurrents in the cavern alerted them to their visitors' presence. The rocks infused with infrared scanned the vehicle, noting three individuals, one male and two females on board. It also registered the beacon, undetectable to human ears, even that of the aliens that had inhibited the earth more than a century ago. The tactical system aboard sent the biometric readings, along with the chemistry makeup and blood work of its passengers, ahead to the watchtower confirming the occupants inside. Once they reach the ten miles from the first perimeter, another vehicle will wait to bring them the rest of the way. Prior to boarding, they will instruct them to shower and change, leaving the articles brought with them on the RV for destruction. The main technician manning the tower picked up the handset and placed a call. "They are here. We are sending the chopper to retrieve them. ETA should be ninety minutes" "Excellent," the voice on the other end responds, "let us prepare for their arrival. Make sure their homes are ready. Before showing them to their quarters, bring Brooks to me."

The announcement system on the RV informs the trio that they are nearing their destination. "When the RV comes to a complete stop, only take the designated wrapped backpack assigned to each of you. Strip to your underwear and leave the clothing you have on inside the RV, along with your socks and shoes. We have placed three individual utility showers for you to wash. It provides clothing and shoes for you in each. Take the underwear and place it in the burn bag. Once done, a helicopter will wait for you in the opening, about three-tenths of a mile to the left of the showers.

 "Welcome home Alexander, Bayja and Brooks. Here is where you will complete the plans to destroy the shadows and jumpstart New Earth." The announcement ends for all but Brooks. In her headset she hears from both her fathers, Morrow (biological) and Worth who had raised her. "Brooks, you will make new alliances. Continue to trust no one. We have given you all the tools and training for the tasks ahead. Wait, watch and listen. You are the chosen leader. There will be many challenges, even by those that become part of your inner circle. You will know what to do when the time is right. Know that we love you. God speed my daughter."

As promised, the RV slows to a small meadow with three aluminum looking closets on the right and another opening on the left. Following the instructions, they undressed and gathered their backpack and left the RV. About sixty steps later, each entered the aluminum closet, showered and changed. As they stepped out of the closet, they noticed the RV had disappeared. Each looked at the other, puzzled, but they spoke no words. They had promised each other prior to leaving the RV that they would not speak another word until they reached their destination. Alexander took the lead as Bayja and Brooks followed through the small opening on the left to the waiting helicopter. The chopper resembled a medevac, military medical helicopter, used to transport medical personnel or injured soldiers back in the late twentieth century. They entered through the side cargo door. There were two individuals dressed in hazard gear waiting. After fastening them in and closing the bay door, the chopper lifts from the ground, going straight up, clearing the trees before turning northeast. From everything they had read about helicopters, the trio noticed they had adjusted the chopper. There was a solid steel fire door that separated the bay from the cockpit. Upon entering the cargo bay, they noticed they darkened the windows of the cockpit, meaning the pilot or pilots could see out, but no one could make out what was inside the aircraft. When the individuals shut the cargo doors, there were no windows. The bay had a seating area for about 10 to 15 individuals. There were also parachutes attached above each seat. They estimated they travelled just above tree level for about thirty minutes before the craft elevated higher as it picked speed. the elevation was subtle, but the trio could tell that the aircraft continued for another thirty minutes before beginning its descent.

Absently, she rubs the pendant at her neck, Brooks closes her eyes while she reflects again on the last conversation before leaving the RV. Meant as a precaution the message was clear and ominous. Her fathers had prepared her as much as they could. Going from taking care of one, to now a colony with at least a few hundred people would be challenging. Her learning curve would fluctuate based on how the colony perceives her, along with Alexander and Bayja. She also had to consider how much of that conversation she would share with Alexander and Bayja. She had to assume that at some point, each received instruction meant for them in order to protect her from going forward. The chopper decreased their speed once more and began a slow, straight down descent. With her eyes still closed, Brooks leaned into her senses, hoping to gain some knowledge that will be useful. Despite not having windows to see out, she could tell from the shadows that there is a section of light to dark. Also, the smell changed as they descended. There was some type of foliage that was not hand crafted. From the speed of the descent, she surmised that the opening or landing space was tight or small. The pilot or pilots made no change forward, backwards, left or right once they continued downward. Opening her eyes, she watched one greeter open the bay door between the cockpit and their seating. There were indeed two people inside. The greeter closed the door behind them, leaving just one greeter still seated with them. Removing the headgear, she sees the gentleman appeared to be around Bayja's age. A thin, fine grade of silver graced his skull and chin. His eyes squarely fixed on her reminded her of a rat, small and darting. He made no move to speak, his gaze taking in her appearance from head to feet. The engine of the chopper stops. He does not move as they continued to sit for another few moments. When he stands, she realizes he shares the same height as Alexander. As he removes his gloves, he extends his hand and moves towards Alexander.

"Welcome Alexander," he starts, "but forgive me, I'm not sure who is Bayja and who is Brooks," he continues as he turns his gaze back to Brooks. Not moving, she answers, "I am Brooks." Turning his direction back to Alexander, he gives his broadest smile, "I am Nikolai. Welcome to Coveia." The side door of the chopper opens and Nikolai steps out, turning, waiting for us to follow. Bayja and Brooks look at each other, wondering if not shaking their hand was intentional to provoke a response to see how tight our union is, or to gauge who he thought was in charge. Grabbing their backpacks, they exit. At first glance, the place resembled the entrance at Quitman Mountains. This was a hanger of sorts. There were five other similar aircraft vehicles, along with a dozen of recalibrated tankers, a few jeeps and several long looking vehicles that past generations referred to as limos. Brooks' mind flashes to the opening in the meadow. Something dark is emerging from the ground, not the Shadows, but something much deadlier that threatens more than just the people in this colony. Its spirit is trying to evade her soul, her thoughts. She feels her energy waning in its attempt to weed itself into her chemistry. Using her telepathic powers, she closes the doors to the chopper and heads towards the cockpit. She empties her thoughts. Her sole focus in drawing the spirit away from her sister,

Alexander, and the immediate platform. Nicholai and others are frantically attempting to open the cargo doors. They are unsuccessful and the sounds of blades continue to whip in fury and the chopper rises from the platform in bolting speed.

"Stop," a lone voice pierces through the whining engines. "she knows what she's doing. Even now, without hesitation, she is protecting her people" Bayja stills as the voice grows closer. A woman, dark as charcoal with silver locs running past her shoulder blades, invades her space. She is towering above her by a good foot. "Welcome, Bayja. Welcome, Alexander. I am Aja Javal, a member of the Head Council of Coveia. We've been expecting you". Extending her hand to Bayja as a sign of peace, she continues, "I knew your father, Morrow, and I were present when both you and Brooks were born. Alexander, do you remember me?" Alexander turns his direction from the chopper moving upward, out of the bay. He sizes Aja up; the memory forming of a nine-year-old boy meeting the charcoal-colored lady, with flaming blue hair and the large catlike eyes, at a rally his parents were attending. "Your hair is no longer blue," he responds. "You will forgive me, but my attention is on my friend here," he continues as he points his finger upward at the chopper now leaving. "Why are you so sure she's protecting her people? Just who are these people?", Bayja inquires pointedly. Aja nods "I understand I have not earned your vote of confidence yet. I am going on intuition that your sister does nothing without a purpose. Please follow me. We must board and leave now". Crossing the deck, they board another similar chopper that leaves westward at a low altitude before gaining upward momentum.

At the throttle, Brooks continues to move the chopper upward. Breathing, she focuses all her thoughts back to the bunker in Winema and the lone man who kept guard above her room. She no longer senses him but another, that just as sinister as the new mystery attempting to overtake her. Tapping into his psyche, she whispers, "I don't think we're alone," hoping the message would reach its intended party. Releasing its hold, the chopper readjusts its course. From the cockpit, Brooks mystified yet drawn to the beauty of the island. The contrast is startling; foliage splashing mixtures of red, purple and orange in full bloom. The sky seemed quite peaceful, clear and full of promises showing no signs on of freakish electrical storms and downpours of frozen boulders coming later. The chopper heads towards the sea, another similar craft in the lead some three hundred yards ahead. Once over the sea, a single voice greets her. "Brooks, my name is Aja Javal. Your sister and Alexander are on board with us and are safe. We thought we would have more time at Coveia to prepare, but another life form has awakened that seems to be more destructive than the Shadows. We must hasten to reach our destination as the storms are approaching from the north are gaining momentum".

"Coveia?" Alex and Bayja respond in unison. Placing a hand on Alexander's thigh, Bayja continues, eyes arched in puzzlement. "I thought we were joining others in Guatemala. Is Coveia a part of that country?" Aja pauses before answering. How long will it take her before she realizes just who is she? Looking at Bayja is like looking at her younger self. She wondered if her daughter had her same personality traits. "No", she starts "we are not going to Guatemala. That was a ploy to bring Jonas out of hiding. I'm glad to say it worked. With him in the open, we can gather more intel on these experiments of his. Find the cure and way to prevent infiltration and destruction from the Shadows. No Coveia is a new region in Africa, founded by the Fathers" She closes her eyes leaving the pair to stew on the information she placed in their laps.

 Aboard her plane, Brooks does not reply. The voice of Aja Javal is familiar to her. It was the same voice she heard every day for three years. Before Alexander. Before meeting her half-sister, Bayja. She had to hand it to her father and Morrows. They were quite thorough in leaving nothing to chance. Not alarming the others, she responds she sees them ahead of her and the foreign object was unsuccessful in trying to penetrate the aircraft. "Wonderful", Aja responds. "Continue to follow us. Put the craft on auto-pilot". She gives the instructions and Brooks relaxes in the cockpit.

From the ground, a lone woman moves with great speed through the jungle. Several minutes earlier she, Baja and Alexander entered the opening, Brooks realizes another life form is present. The same that laid dormant at Aeverless and Ground Zero. This continuous game of chess becoming more deadly with each move. unknown to her sister and Alexander, a living AI, lived within her. She activated the remaining android, an exact duplicate of her, prior to leaving the RV. It traveled with them invisibly until this very moment. From her hiding place, Brooks watched it board the chopper along with the unknown alien, Alexander and her sister. Once again, she is alone. The timer in the cockpit will explode in a few hours before reaching its ultimate destination. Whatever it is, it will not survive to inflict the remaining. It is imperative that they reach their destination with the belief that she died from a malfunction on the other chopper. For now, they must not become privy to that fact that there is another life form, deadlier than the Shadows on board with the android. This moment, her responsibility remains here. Unsure of where here is, she continues traveling inward, knowing she only has a few hours before dark to reach her destination.

In a matter of a few months, she left the comfort of Aeverless to the outer shores of Oregon, Alaska. Her companions, Alexander and Baja, are heading to the continent of Africa, to the unknown world named Coveia. She had only seen pictures of Africa. She wondered if they spared the continent the ravages of what she saw in North America, barren cold stretches of land, black, frigid, steeped in deep mist and unimaginable horrors. If there were any creatures in the sea, from the submarine they were undetectable and for that she is grateful. She could not imagine what they would encounter. Would it be friendly or dangerous territory? That was the least of their worries. This latest hap stance on the island; another unknown life force totally undetectable until seconds before it strikes. Was this an off breed of the Shadows or a new predator? She is quite certain that neither her father nor Morrows knew about this, and if so, did they realize the threat? Either way, this is a new wrinkle of the worst imaginable kind.

~

Jonas' vital signs continued to deteriorate. Whatever mixture of gases concocted here was quite effective. His ability to mind meld was as useless as his ability to move at the moment. Somehow, he wills himself to try after hearing the whisper, the girl, warn him they were not alone. It took him more than an hour to move from his last location and prop himself up at the console. He is oblivious to the black gunk oozing down the walls; the tentacles moving across the floor. His eyes are focusing on the flashing red light at the console. Mustering his strength, his finger lands on the light as the substance engulfs his body at a fervent pace. In less than a minute it cocoons his entire body, like a moth, and the light distinguishes.

THE END

Stay tuned for Aeverless 3.2 The Rise of the Shadows, coming fall 2021.

Meet the characters of Aeverless

BAYJA

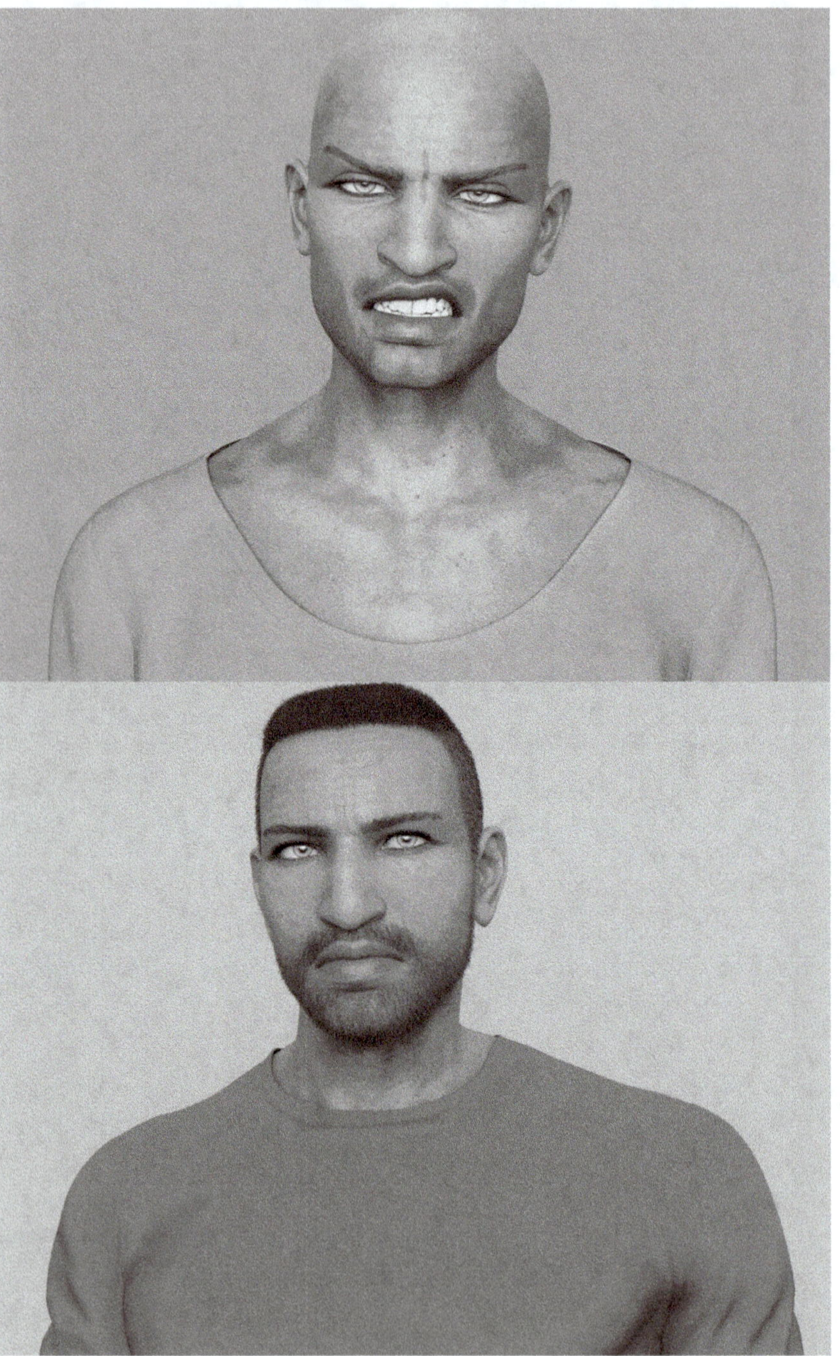

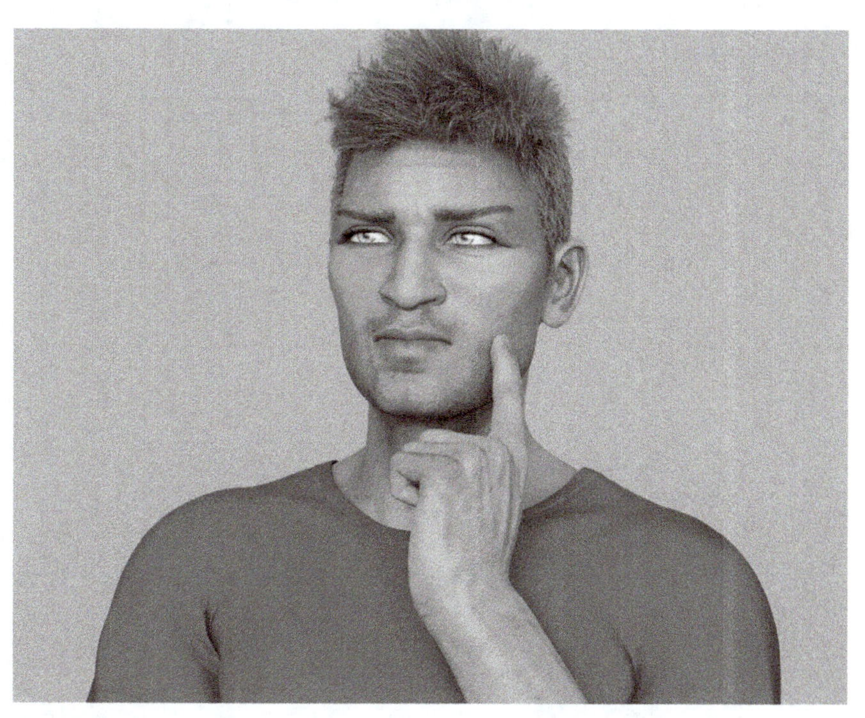

Meet the Author

Meet the Author

Jones Harwell

Worked as a telecommunications specialist for over thirty years in private industry, academia and as a federal contractor. A wife and mother of two children and glam-ma to three grandchildren, she holds a BA in Communication Studies and a graduate degree in Early Childhood Studies. When not spending time with family and friends, writing, cooking or listening to music, you can find her volunteering in her community in state of Maryland.

In 2019, Lisa founded Redbaby Publishing, Inc. with the release of her first novel The Chameleon. In fulfilling a childhood dream, she realized that writing became her purpose and platform to help other individuals document their stories. Visit her website at jonesharwell.com to learn more about the author, publisher, journalist and pod caster.

www.ingramcontent.com/pod-product-compliance
Lightning Source LLC
Chambersburg PA
CBHW071804190726

48292CB00008B/2706